A Saxon Shadow

A SAXON SHADOW

A CHIEF INSPECTOR SHADOW MYSTERY

H L Marsay

TULE
PUBLISHING

DEDICATION

In memory of my lovely grandparents,

Lily and Leslie Robinson.

CHAPTER ONE

Across 9 (5 letters)
Did Ralph rive this waterway?

I T WAS A perfect spring day. The sun was shining in the cloudless blue sky, warming the cool March air. Chief Inspector John Shadow had taken a seat outside the Duke of York, one of his favourite pubs. He had a pint of Theakston's in his hand, the half-finished *Yorkshire Post* crossword was on the table in front of him and a waitress was heading towards him with a steak and onion sandwich. It would have been close to his idea of heaven if it wasn't for the presence of a busker a few feet away from him. King's Square, like the other city squares in York, was a magnet for street entertainers, with varying degrees of talent. This particular busker had taken up position on the old graveyard, the raised platform was all that remained of the church that had once stood there. He was wearing a dark blue frock coat, an eyepatch, a tricorn hat and a toy parrot attached to his shoulder. He also had an accordion that he was playing very loudly as he belted out a series of sea shanties and folk songs.

"He must be lost. We're miles from the coast," muttered

Shadow as he tried to concentrate on the next clue.

"Are you enjoying the music?" asked the young waitress as she placed his lunch in front of him. He looked up at her innocent smile. She wasn't being sarcastic.

"Will he be here long?" he asked.

She shrugged. "Probably. They can stay for a maximum of two hours, and he's only just started. Enjoy your lunch."

Shadow sighed as he cut into his sandwich and tried to ignore the noise, but it was impossible. Within a few minutes, a group of excitable schoolchildren on a visit to York's Chocolate Story had gathered around him and were demanding he play "What shall we do with a drunken sailor?" When they'd gone, he started on "The Wild Rover", now accompanied by an elderly lady dancing around her shopping trolley. Shadow couldn't take any more. He finished his last mouthful of sandwich, threw back the remains of his pint, tucked his paper under his arm and stalked away.

As it was such a pleasant afternoon, he decided to take a stroll through Museum Gardens. At least there wouldn't be any buskers there. There was nothing on his desk that required his attention except for a large document the chief constable had sent to him with the ominous title: "Continuous Improvement Self-Assessment Matrix". That could definitely be ignored for a few more days. Unusually, Jimmy Chang—his sergeant—hadn't bothered him all day either. He was meant to be gathering evidence regarding a spate of burglaries that had taken place in and around the city over the past few weeks. It was therefore with some surprise that when Shadow arrived in the gardens, he spotted his sergeant standing outside the Yorkshire Museum.

"What are you doing here?" he asked by way of a greeting.

"Afternoon, Chief. We got called out to a report of vandalism. Tom was covering the front desk and knew I was in the area, so he asked me to attend. Someone has been digging in the old abbey," explained Jimmy, removing his sunglasses and gesturing to the ruins of St Mary's Abbey. It had once been one of the largest Benedictine monasteries in the country, but now little remained except the crumbling walls of the nave and some gravestones.

"Any damage?" asked Shadow.

"No, at least nothing the gardeners can't fix. Four were holes dug near where the altar once stood apparently. The warden thinks it might be metal detectorists. He said there's a group of them who are always trying to sneak in."

"How?" asked Shadow. He couldn't imagine anyone scaling the garden walls, especially not if they were burdened with metal detectors and spades.

Jimmy shrugged. "The warden said he got called out at about seven o'clock last night. Someone living in one of the flats across the road saw a light moving around. It must have been the intruder's torch. The warden entered by the gates on St Mary's but when he arrived, whoever it was had gone.

How come you're here? I thought you'd be having lunch."

"That was the plan until the busking started," grumbled Shadow.

"Oh dear. Was it the morris dancers?" asked Jimmy sympathetically.

"No, some idiot dressed up like Long John Silver singing sea shanties."

Jimmy shook his head. "He must be a new one. I haven't seen him."

"Think yourself lucky," he replied rummaging in his pocket for an indigestion tablet and cursing the busker once more for making him rush his lunch. "How did it go at the bank?"

The only thing that seemed to connect the burglaries they were investigating was the fact that all the break-ins had occurred while the homeowners were away on holiday. Jimmy had spent the morning following up on a theory that there could be a link between where the victims had bought their foreign currency. All four of them had used the same bank, albeit different branches.

"Nothing concrete but the cashier who served the first two victims was Dani Piper. It was euros for the old farmer from Sheriff Hutton and US dollars for the couple from the big house outside Strensall."

Shadow frowned. He knew that name.

"Tyson Piper's wife?" he asked.

"His sister."

"Is he out?" asked Shadow. Tyson had been convicted of credit card fraud and sentenced to six years, but he couldn't quite remember when.

"No and his sister—technically half-sister—doesn't have a record to be fair, but I thought it was worth noting. Although Dani has never worked in either the Malton or Thirsk branch, so then if she did turn out to be dodgy, it wouldn't really fit with the other two burglaries."

"Unless one of her colleagues is involved too," mused Shadow but, at that moment, Jimmy's phone began to bleep. Shadow turned away while his sergeant took the call. He wandered over to look at the tulips that were blooming amongst the ruins. In the distance, he could see a team of gardeners working on the area that must have been dug up. A squirrel scampered along the high garden wall and Shadow again wondered how the metal detectorists or whoever it was managed to climb over without anyone noticing. His thoughts were interrupted by Jimmy.

"Report of a burglary out near Whitby, Chief," he said cheerfully.

"Why are they phoning you? Can't they deal with it?"

"It sounds like it might be another one for us. Smashed window to gain entry. Cash and electronics taken. The owner is away on holiday and his sister called to report the break-in this morning."

"A trip to the coast it is then," replied Shadow, thinking the chief constable's missive could gather dust a bit longer.

"Excellent!" said Jimmy, sliding his sunglasses—which Shadow suspected were expensive and designer—back on. "We could get fish and chips while we're there."

"Maybe," replied Shadow, but from the grumbling sounds it was making, his stomach didn't agree.

SHADOW CHEWED SEVERAL more indigestion tablets, while Jimmy drove like a maniac for thirty minutes and without being asked provided an update to his personal life. Sophie, his wife and one of the pathologists they worked with, had returned to the family farm after her father had suffered a stroke. She was hopeful he would make a full recovery, but she would be away for a few days, which meant their house hunting had been put on hold. His sergeant and Sophie had been unsuccessfully looking for a new place to live since they got married, and it seemed to be becoming an obsession with Jimmy. As he pondered aloud the pros and cons of leasehold and freehold, Shadow merely nodded and gave the occasional grunt as he gripped his seat with one hand and the door with the other.

As it turned out, the burglary wasn't in Whitby itself, but in Ellerdale, a village on the edge of the moors and about ten minutes from the coast, but then geography had never been Jimmy's strong point. Ellerdale was a large village, with a collection of shops and pubs arranged around a cobbled market square. A pretty beck flowed around the back of the ancient church that sat next to a row of stone cottages.

The address they had been given, Camelot Cottage, was the last and largest property in this row. They parked in front of the garden gate. There was nothing to show something was amiss except for the presence of a nervous-looking young woman in the uniform of a police community support officer. She was standing on guard outside the front door.

"If this is a crime scene, shouldn't it be taped off?" asked Shadow, after introducing himself and Jimmy. The PCSO, whose name was Natalie Sharp, turned red.

"Yes, sir. It was. At least, we started to tape it off, but then Reverend Prescott came by and asked us if we wouldn't mind taking it down again. You see, Ellerdale is in the regional final for England's Perfect Village. The judges don't give any warning when they are coming but it could be any day now and the reverend thought it might not be a good look to see police tape everywhere. Sergeant Thornton said it would be okay, as long as I stayed here and didn't let anyone in until you arrived." She was beginning to stammer now as she rushed her words. Shadow held up his hand to stop her.

"All right, thank you. What can you tell us about the break-in?" he asked.

Looking relieved, she whipped her electronic notebook out of her pocket at exactly the same time Jimmy produced his and began to read.

"The house belongs to Mr Lance Debenham. His sister,

Miss Alice Debenham, reported the break-in at 8.45am this morning."

"Has Mr Debenham lived here long?" asked Shadow. A slight look of confusion crossed Natalie's face.

"The Debenhams have always lived in Ellerdale, sir."

"I see. Does Miss Debenham live here too?" asked Shadow.

"No, sir. Mr Debenham is on holiday. His sister was here to feed his cat, Merlin."

"Camelot Cottage and Merlin the cat. I take it Mr Debenham is a fan of Arthurian legend?" However, his comment was met with blank stares from his two younger colleagues. "I'll let you tell Sergeant Chang the rest, while I take a look inside," he continued.

Shadow left the two devotees of the electronic notepad to discuss the case and instead stepped through the front door, ducking his head beneath the low frame. It was dark and cool inside the cottage. The floor was polished stone, and the walls were painted white. An oak settle and a longcase clock stood at the bottom of the narrow stairs. He made his way from the hall into the sitting room. Cushions from the two sofas had been thrown on the floor, a collection of carefully framed antique maps were now hanging on the wall at strange angles and the contents of the drawers in the polished oak desk had been emptied out. As far as he could tell nothing was smashed or broken.

After retracing his steps he went upstairs. There were

three bedrooms and a bathroom. All were in utter disarray. Bedding had been flung on the floor, wardrobe doors and drawers were open, and clothes scattered around. The full laundry basket had been knocked over and its contents gave off a damp, sweaty odour. Even the bathroom cupboard had been ransacked. Shadow paused for a moment to examine the razors and tubes of toothpaste lying in the sink. He would hazard a guess that Mr Debenham lived alone.

He went back downstairs and walked through to the kitchen. Again, cupboards and drawers had been opened but there didn't appear to be any breakages except for a small pane of glass in one of the leaded windows that overlooked the rear garden. The window was wide open, and it looked like that was how the intruder had gained access. Shadow went over to take a closer look then quickly stepped back as a large fluffy grey cat who had been sitting on the sill behind the curtain sprang down with a hiss. He arched his back and glared at Shadow as he walked by swishing his tail.

"Hey, this must be Merlin," said Jimmy as he arrived in the kitchen and immediately knelt down to fuss over the now purring puss. "Poor thing! I wonder if the intruder upset him."

"Any thoughts on the break-in rather than the welfare of the cat?" asked Shadow tetchily. Jimmy stood up and consulted his notebook.

"Well, it's not exactly like the other ones, Chief. Three of the others had the lock on the back doors forced. Only one had a window broken to gain access, like here. It must have been a tight squeeze," he added gesturing to the open window. "And another thing—this place has been left in a real mess too. I've had a quick look upstairs and all the bedding and mattresses have been pulled off the beds. At the others, it seemed like the burglars were more methodical, like they knew what they were looking for. The four other houses all had loads of high-value tech taken and expensive watches and cash. And the other four were all in fairly remote locations without any near neighbours so nobody could hear anything. Natalie said she had spoken to the neighbours, and nobody heard anything here either. Although, they are both quite elderly, apparently. One wears a hearing aid and they both went to bed at half past nine. The property on the other side of them is a holiday cottage and the family who own it aren't here at the moment. Really, the only thing that's similar to the other break-ins is that the owner had gone on holiday when it happened."

"Is there an alarm?" asked Shadow.

Jimmy shook his head. "No. Actually, the other four didn't have alarms either. That's another similarity, I suppose."

Shadow nodded although, like his sergeant, he wasn't entirely convinced this crime was linked to the others. Something about it felt different.

"Do we know what's been taken yet?" he asked.

"Well, we can't be sure until Mr Debenham returns.

He's been contacted and he's on his way back home. Apparently, he's due anytime."

"That's quick. Where's he coming back from?"

"Well, that's another difference, Chief. The other victims had all gone on holiday abroad, but he was only up north somewhere," replied Jimmy who was still scrolling through his notes. "Re missing items, again different to the other break-in. Mr Debenham's sister said that biscuit tin over there always had about thirty or forty quid in it to pay the milkman or the window cleaner and that's empty now." He gestured to a small tin that was lying empty on the floor, then turned his attention back to his notes. "There were two bottles of rhubarb gin on the sideboard in the sitting room. Alice Debenham makes it herself and she said they are both missing."

"Sounds disgusting," muttered Shadow as Jimmy continued.

"Also, there was a computer on the desk in the sitting room and that's gone, but the sister described it as pretty ancient."

"Where is she now?"

"In the garden, Chief. Meditating."

They found Alice Debenham sitting cross-legged on the grass beneath a cherry tree. Her hands were resting on her knees, her eyes were closed and her long grey hair was held back with two wooden combs. She was dressed in a long denim skirt with a pale pink shirt and an embroidered waistcoat. There were several silver chains with Celtic pendants hanging around her neck and the backs of her hands were adorned with henna swirls. Her face was make-up free and serene. Shadow gave a small cough as they approached, and her eyes sprang open.

"I'm sorry to disturb you, Miss Debenham," he began. "This is Sergeant Chang, and I am Chief Inspector Shadow."

"And a Scorpio if I'm not mistaken," she said looking him up and down, before turning her pale blue gaze to Jimmy. "Ah and you are definitely an air sign. Gemini? Libra?"

"Libra. How did you know?"

"You have an aura about you. We all do. Luckily, I'm very sensitive to auras. It's one of my many gifts. I also read palms." She reached out and took Jimmy's hand. "Ah, I see there has been sadness in your life, but the future looks bright. Your heartline is very deep. That means you are in tune with your emotions." She tapped his wedding ring, "I would expect you to have a long and happy marriage."

Jimmy looked delighted. "Really? That's amazing. What else can you see?"

Shadow had to suppress a groan. If it wasn't for Jimmy's note-taking ability, he sometimes thought he'd be better working alone. It would certainly be quicker. He cleared his throat.

"I understand you discovered the break-in this morning, Miss Debenham."

"You fire signs. So impatient," she replied with a little chuckle as she dropped Jimmy's hand. "Yes, I arrived here at half past eight. The church clock was striking as I walked up the path."

"You entered through the front door?"

"That's right. Lance dropped off a key for me before he left on Friday."

"Did you see or hear anything unusual when you arrived?"

"No everything looked as it should, but I did have a sense something untoward had happened. There was a definite disturbance in the atmosphere. I only knew something was wrong for sure when I stepped inside and saw all the mess. And before you ask, no I didn't touch anything. Oh except for giving Merlin a reassuring stroke—and I picked up the petty cash tin and I had to touch the telephone obviously."

"To call your brother?" asked Shadow.

"Yes, I phoned him first. He's on his way home but he insisted I call the police and wait for them to arrive, which was rather a nuisance as I had to cancel this morning's class."

"Class?" asked Jimmy, who was diligently taking notes again.

"Yes, I hold a class once a week in the village hall. Nature's Bounty—Herbs and How to Use Them. Today we were going to be making our own tea blends." She produced a small drawstring muslin bag from her pocket and opened it to reveal what looked like dried twigs and grass. "This is my personal favourite. Vanilla and chamomile along with my secret ingredient."

Jimmy leant down to take a sniff. "That smells great."

"And very calming. Perfect for a stressful situation. I would offer to make you both a cup but your rather officious colleague told me a hundred times not to touch anything. Honestly, I remember her as a little girl, playing in the beck. A bit of power goes completely to some people's heads. I blame the uniform."

"Are you able to tell us what may have been taken, Miss Debenham?" asked Shadow, keen to get back on track. He had no intention of drinking anything she brewed. He'd stick to Yorkshire tea.

Alice shrugged. "I already told Natalie. Some cash, some booze, a rather ancient computer. Ah! Here's Lance now. I'm sure he'll be able to answer all your questions," she said waving to a tall, thin man who was striding across the lawn with Merlin the cat tucked under his arm. As he approached, Alice walked away in the opposite direction to a small gate at the bottom of the garden.

"Sorry about the break-in Lance," she called over her shoulder. "They've made quite a mess. Hope you get it cleared up," she added before disappearing from view.

As well as sharing his sister's tall slim build, Lance Debenham also had the same pale blue eyes as Alice. However, where Alice had a willowy almost ethereal air about her,

Lance seemed far more robust. He was dressed in a fleece top with an anorak over it and his Lycra cycling shorts showed off his muscular calves. His face was tanned and his still-blond hair was brushed back. A pair of wire-rimmed spectacles balanced precariously on the end of his long thin nose. It was through these glasses that he squinted at the detective's ID as Shadow introduced himself and Jimmy.

"Shadow? Excellent name derived from both Middle English and Old English," declared Lance then switched his attention to Jimmy's warrant card.

"Chang," he read. "Oh well, never mind." He turned to Shadow again. "I've only had a quick look inside, but my sister is correct, the place looks like a bomb has hit it. I can't understand it. This sort of thing never happens in Ellerdale. However, while I'm flattered you are here, I'm rather surprised that a chief inspector is investigating my break-in."

"We have reason to believe that there could be a connection to some other incidents we have been investigating. I understand you've lived in Ellerdale all your life, Mr Debenham."

"You understand correctly, Chief Inspector. The Debenhams have always lived in Ellerdale. In fact, we were mentioned in the Domesday Book. We owned most of the village then." When neither Shadow nor Jimmy looked impressed by this information, he continued. "I teach history and geography at a boys prep school in Oxfordshire, but I always return here for the hols."

"Who looks after Merlin while you're away?" asked Jimmy.

Lance looked at him with disdain. Shadow thought if he was the casting director for a film set in the Second World War, Mr Debenham would be perfect as a Gestapo officer.

"Merlin comes to school with me. I'm the master in charge of Hereward House. The boys are very fond of him."

"Do you live here alone, Mr Debenham?" asked Shadow.

"Yes. This used to be my parents' home. Alice and I grew up here. I inherited it when my father died."

"And you were away on holiday when the break-in occurred."

"Yes, I left on Friday morning."

"Were you going anywhere nice?" asked Jimmy.

"A two-week cycling tour of Northumbria."

"Really? My wife's from round there. Great beaches."

A haughty look appeared on Lance's face.

"I was going on a pilgrimage to Lindisfarne. I try to go there at least once a year to commemorate the lives of the monks who were so brutally massacred by the heathen Vikings. The timing was intentional as it's close to the anniversary of the Battle of York in 867 when the brave kings Aella and Osberht led a counter-attack against the army of the Vikings who had occupied the city. Alas, as they breached the city's defences, they were slain bringing an end to the Anglo-Saxon Kingdom of Northumbria and paving the way for the creation of Jorvik. A sad day, I'm sure you will agree."

"You got back from Lindisfarne very quickly," said Shadow, who really didn't appreciate the distraction of a history lecture.

"I was in Durham when I received the news from Alice. I left here on Friday and cycled to Ripon where I spent the evening. Over the weekend, I was in Bishop Auckland and reached Durham yesterday. I planned to spend two nights there and visit the shrine to the Venerable Bede. After all, it is thanks to him we know so much about our country before it was ransacked by the Danes and their ancestors the Normans. However, it seems I must forgo or at least post-pone my annual visit. I caught the train back to Whitby as soon as Alice telephoned me."

"Did you cycle from the station?" asked Jimmy.

Another supercilious look crossed Lance's face. "General-ly, I cycle everywhere, Sergeant," he replied. "However, with the shock of hearing my home had been broken into, I forgot to collect my bike. It's still in the store at the Airbnb I was renting in Durham. It's most irritating. I took a taxi from the station."

"Are you able to tell us what has been taken?" asked Shadow as Jimmy continued to note all these details down.

Lance gave a slight shrug. "As I said, I've only had a brief look. Natalie told me not to touch anything until your CSI chaps have been in. There was a rather ancient laptop on my desk. That's gone and some bottles of gin too, but I can't be sure of anything else. The place has been completely ran-sacked."

"Your sister mentioned a quantity of cash was also miss-ing," said Shadow.

Lance frowned. "Did she? As I said, I haven't checked thoroughly." His tone was more irritated than upset.

"Who knew you were going away?" asked Shadow.

Lance gave the two detectives another contemptuous look. Shadow wondered whether he had a particular dislike of police officers or if after years of teaching twelve- and thirteen-year-old boys this had become his default facial expression. Or was it that he simply preferred to be the one asking the questions? Either way, he was finding it increas-ingly difficult to have any sympathy for the man, burglary or no burglary.

"I discussed my plans with Alice and a couple of friends in the village. I also cancelled my regular milk delivery. However, I'm sure if anyone was watching the house, they would have seen me leave with a large holdall and made their own assumptions. Now if you will both excuse me, I would like to return to Whitby and speak to my insurance brokers. I expect they'll need a crime number from you. Then I shall have to try to find someone to fix the window before it rains. I also want to take Merlin to the vets for a check-up. This whole business must have been very upsetting for him."

Shadow didn't think the fluffy grey cat looked remotely perturbed, but merely nodded as Lance and Merlin disappeared back into the house. Shadow waited until they were out of sight before speaking. "It seems strange he forgot his bike, don't you think?" he asked. "He's even wearing cycling gloves."

Jimmy shook his head. "Not really, Chief. Like he said, he heard he'd been burgled and panicked."

"He didn't seem the panicking type," replied Shadow. "You had better sort out a crime number for him as soon as possible though." He pointed to the broken window. "Let's take a closer look over there. Have the local police called CSI or forensics out?"

"Natalie said she was told to wait for us to arrive, so I called out our teams from York—you know in case it is connected to the other burglaries."

They made their way over to the open kitchen window. Shadow knelt down and carefully inspected the flower bed. The tulips and late-flowering daffodils had been trodden down, but he couldn't see any footprints, although it had been unusually dry recently. Glinting amongst the blades of grass were a few shards of glass. He was about to mention them to Jimmy when Natalie appeared again looking flustered.

"Sorry to interrupt, sir, but a man's been found. Or rather a body has been. He's dead. We'd normally contact Northallerton, but Sergeant Thornton said seeing as you are here." She shook her head. "I don't understand it, sir. Nothing ever usually happens here and now a burglary and poor Dr Underhill on the same day." Her hand flew to her mouth. "Mr Debenham was his best friend. Should I tell him before he leaves?"

Shadow felt sure that if Lance was still inside the cottage, he would have heard their discussion, but he shook his head.

"Not until we've informed the dead man's family. Where is the body?"

Natalie looked confused. "At Underhill's Mill. Like I said, it's Dr Underhill. Kenelm Underhill."

She spoke with the expectation that the two detectives would know the name of the dead man, but it meant nothing to Shadow. He looked over to his sergeant. Jimmy had a frown on his face, which quickly turned into a look of recognition.

"Underhills. The people who make the biscuits for dogs and cats. Fawkes loves their salmon-flavoured ones," he explained referring to his cat.

"That's right, sir," agreed Constable Sharp. "Underhills have been milling animal feed for centuries."

"Where is this mill from here?"

"Just up the road, sir, but…" she hesitated "…but I heard on the radio that the road is blocked. Some sheep have escaped from their field and are loose in the marketplace. You might be quicker walking. If you go through the gate at the bottom of the garden and follow the path down by the beck past the church, you'll be there in about ten minutes."

The two detectives did as Natalie suggested and walked

through the same small wooden gate at the bottom of the garden that Alice had left by. They stepped on to a narrow path that led through the woods and along the gently flowing beck. It was cool in the shade and there was a strong smell of wild garlic. They passed the back of the church as the path continued to slowly slope downwards and the beck gradually grew a little wider and the current ran a little faster.

"Chief, did you think it was weird that Alice didn't stick around? You'd think she'd offer to help him clear up," said Jimmy.

"I'm more concerned with a possible connection between the break-in and this dead body. According to Natalie nothing ever happens here and now Mr Debenham's house is burgled, and his best friend is dead," replied Shadow.

After about five minutes, the trees became less dense, and the mill came into view.

It was an imposing stone building about four storeys high. A range of low buildings also made of stone ran to the left and then turned at a right angle, and then turned again to form a courtyard. Attached to the mill on the right-hand side was a large timber-framed house. The stone above the front door was dated 1603. Both buildings were so old and crooked they looked like they were holding each other up. They veered off the path and walked up to the main gateway, passed some stables to where two marked police cars were parked in the courtyard.

Shadow was relieved to see the local police had managed

to secure this site. Blue and white tape that ran in front of both the house and the mill. A short, stout uniformed sergeant came bustling towards them, his face flushed and his arms full of protective covers for their shoes and gloves.

"Chief Inspector Shadow? Sergeant Chang? I'm Sergeant Thornton, sir. I'm sorry we don't have any protective suits. I got the lads from Whitby to bring this stuff over with them," he explained nodding to the two young constables standing by the second patrol car. "But we haven't touched anything, except to check he was definitely dead."

"That's fine, Sergeant. Where is the body?" asked Shadow, as he covered his shoes and pulled on the gloves.

"Kenelm's in his study. It looks like whoever did it broke in through the garden door. I'll take you round there."

"And who found him?" asked Shadow as they followed Sergeant Thornton back to the path by the beck.

"Glenda Kemp, Kenelm's housekeeper. She's in the kitchen but she's badly shaken up."

"What can you tell us about the dead man?" asked Shadow as they walked along.

"Let me see now, Chief Inspector," replied Sergeant Thornton scratching his head, "Kenelm was a few years behind me at school, so he must be around fifty-two now. He's lived here in the village all his life, except when he went away to school and university. He inherited the mill when his father died. He was a bit of an eccentric, but then his kind often are."

Shadow nodded, although he wasn't sure what the sergeant was alluding to. "Is he a medical doctor?"

"No. He's one of them university-type doctors."

"What in?" he asked assuming it would be a PhD in agriculture or food production.

"I'm not totally sure, sir, but it'll be something to do with history. That's all he's ever been interested in."

"Like his friend, Lance Debenham?" asked Jimmy.

"Oh yes, Sergeant Chang. Thick as thieves those two were. They were born only a few days apart. They maybe aren't quite as close as they once were, but this will be quite a blow to poor Lance. First his house being robbed and now this," he continued, almost repeating what Natalie had said.

The path led them to a wooden gate similar to the one at Camelot Cottage. This gate was also marked *private* and had a sign saying *Mill House*. There was a bolt but no lock. As Sergeant Thornton opened the gate for them, Shadow took a moment to survey the garden. It was large and sweeping and it sloped upwards away from the beck. There were little gravel and stone paths twisting between the large rhododendrons and apple trees past various seating areas carved out of stone and up to the house.

"Is this the only way into the garden from outside the house?" he asked.

"That's right, sir," replied Sergeant Thornton. "Follow me. I'll show you the way."

They made slow progress behind the huffing and puffing

sergeant, but eventually reached the terrace at the back of the house. One area of the pale-yellow flagstones was covered with shards of glass where a pair of French doors had been smashed.

"We reckon that's how they got in. It's Kenelm's study through there. We had a quick check, and it doesn't look like any other room has been disturbed," panted their guide as he flopped down on to a metal patio chair. Shadow left him to catch his breath and stepped into the study, wondering why the criminals had felt the need to smash both doors.

Kenelm Underhill lay in a crumpled heap on the floor. There was a small gash on his right temple that had crusted over with dried blood. If Shadow had been guessing, he would have said he was in his late sixties at least. A thin man of average height. He looked to be wearing his pyjamas with a leather tunic over the top and a paisley scarf knotted around his neck. On his feet were a pair of leather slippers. He had shoulder-length grey hair and a straggly grey beard. His skin looked dry and parched. It was hard to believe he and Lance Debenham were the same age.

"Any chance you think he could have fallen?" asked Jimmy.

"It's possible I suppose, but he would have needed to hit his head on something to cause it to bleed," replied Shadow. "You'd better get in touch with CSI and forensics. Tell them to come here instead of the cottage. That will have to wait for now."

"Maybe this was a burglary too, but it went wrong. Mr Underhill disturbed the intruder and he attacked him," suggested Jimmy as he pulled his phone out of his pocket.

"Maybe," sighed Shadow as he surveyed the room. It had wood-panelled walls with a low-beamed ceiling.

A thick red carpet covered the floor and matching heavy velvet curtains hung at windows with leaded light panes like those at Camelot Cottage. Also like the cottage, the walls were covered in framed old maps of the area and architectural drawings. On closer inspection, Shadow saw they were of the inside of various churches and cathedrals. On the oak sideboard was a silver tray holding a couple of glasses but no decanter or bottles of alcohol. A large desk dominated the rest of the room, and it was covered in papers and more maps. Half a dozen glass cabinets, like those found in museums, contained various bits of pottery and metal work. None of the cabinets were damaged but some crockery on a wooden tray had been smashed.

Several framed photographs were also scatted on the floor along with a table lamp and cushions from the two armchairs that stood on either side of the fireplace. Shadow picked up one of the photographs. It showed a group of young people having a picnic out on the moors somewhere. There was a pile of stones behind them. Shadow thought it could be somewhere near Whitby. It looked like it had been taken about thirty years ago. He was fairly certain that the man in the middle was Kenelm and to his left was a young man laughing and holding a bottle of champagne. He didn't know who the woman wearing a rather fixed grin standing behind them was, but Kenelm definitely had his arm wrapped around a young Alice Debenham. She had barely changed, except her brown, henna streaked hair was now grey.

Shadow sniffed. There was a faint smell he thought he recognised but at that moment, he was distracted by a whimpering sound. He turned around. The door that led into the corridor had a child gate on it and on the other side was a black dog with a white stripe on his face. He was lying down, his soulful eyes peering through the bars of the gate. He let out a whimper when Shadow looked at him.

"Hush, Badger," chided Sergeant Thornton who had caught his breath and rejoined them.

"Does Dr Underhill have young children?" Shadow would have thought he was too old but you never knew these days. "Or grandchildren?"

"No. The child gate is for Badger. He's a bit boisterous. According to Glenda, Kenelm had some precious document or other he was working on, and he didn't want to risk Badger destroying it. He's got form apparently: two cushions, a slipper and a copy of the *Daily Telegraph*. Kenelm tried shutting him out, but he made a right mess of the door." He pointed the deep scratch marks at the base of the solid wood door. "The vet said it was separation anxiety. It was Glenda's idea to use a child gate. He was calm as long as he could still see his master. Pity he couldn't get over to protect him last night."

Jimmy went over to stroke the miserable canine. "If only you could talk eh, boy," he said softly.

Shadow frowned. "Surely if he was here when the intruder broke in, he'd have barked the house down. Didn't anyone hear anything? The housekeeper?"

"Oh Glenda doesn't live in. She's got a cottage in the village behind the Bull. She said she went home at about seven o'clock last night and normally she would come over in the morning to make Mr Underhill his breakfast, but Tuesdays are her grocery shopping days, so she went to the supermarket in Whitby and had a few errands to run too, dry cleaners and the like," explained the sergeant.

Shadow nodded thinking he seemed to have collected rather a lot of information from the housekeeper who was supposed to be badly shaken up. He was about to ask to speak with her, but the sergeant was still talking.

"Then Trevor, the security guard, well he knocked off at about ten and went to the pub for a quick pint before last orders but he says it was all quiet on the Western Front. That was a little joke. Not that he meant any disrespect," he explained to Jimmy who was noting everything down. "Incidentally, Trevor's in the kitchen with Glenda, if you want to speak to him."

"That's great, thanks," replied Jimmy. "Do you know Trevor's second name?"

"Yes, it's Thornton and no relation before you ask. Just a coincidence," the sergeant said with a chuckle. "There's quite a few of us around these parts."

"So Dr Underhill lived here alone?" asked Shadow not wanting to be distracted by details of the sergeant's family tree.

"No, Mrs Underhill lives here as well but I haven't seen her yet, I'm afraid." He paused and frowned. "Come to think of it, it's a bit odd she didn't find him, isn't it? Although, and I'm not one to gossip, but they do say theirs isn't the happiest of marriages."

"What about the mill employees?" asked Shadow.

"They would all have left by five thirty yesterday, except for Trevor, and after Kenelm was found all the staff were sent home, but I've got a list of their names and addresses from Mr Underhill," he said removing a folded-up sheet of paper from his pocket and handing it over to Jimmy, who nodded gratefully.

"Mr Underhill?" asked Shadow.

"Oh yes, I should have said, Mr Edmund Underhill. Kenelm's younger brother. He works here too, but he doesn't live here."

At that moment, there was a noise farther down the corridor. Raised voices and heavy footsteps, then a tall thin man wearing a navy pinstriped suit appeared. He had sharp features and his dark hair flopped across his face as he lowered his head to clear the beams.

"What the hell is going on?" he demanded.

"Mr Underhill, we did ask you stay outside, sir," said Sergeant Thornton.

"Whilst at the same time telling me my brother is dead. Do you expect me to do nothing? Sit, Badger!" he snapped at the dog who had stood up to greet him, then noticing the body on the floor. "Good God! What happened? Was he attacked? Did he fall?"

"Was your brother in the habit of falling over, sir?" asked Shadow. Edmund Underhill turned away from his brother and scowled at him. Shadow realised he was the young man with the champagne in the photo.

"Who the hell are you?" he asked.

"I'm Chief Inspector Shadow and this is Detective Sergeant Chang. We'll be leading the investigation into your brother's death. We're very sorry for your loss."

"Thank you. I'm pleased to see they've sent someone competent to take charge," replied Edmund Underhill as Sergeant Thornton turned pink. Edmund gestured to his brother. "Can't you cover him up? His eyes are still open for God's sake."

"I'm sorry, sir. We can't touch the body until the pathologist and the forensics team have seen him. They're on their way. Can you tell me when you last saw your brother?"

"It must have been some time yesterday afternoon. Around three, I think. I brought some papers across to him in here. They needed his signature."

"Did you think it was strange when you didn't see him this morning? Don't the two of you work together?"

"Kenelm's the chairman of Underhill's Mill but he's never been exactly hands on, Chief Inspector. I deal with the day-to-day running of the place. He spent most of his time in here working on this nonsense." He waved dismissively at the documents and maps strewn across the desk and sneered. "Kenelm was obsessed by the Saxons and the Angles or whatever they are called. He was always trying to unearth some bit of history nobody else had discovered. Utter waste of time."

"Lance Debenham is also interested in the Anglo-Saxons, I believe," replied Shadow.

Edmund sneered again. "The two of them are as bad as each other. Boring as buggery. They've been best friends all their lives. They even set up a Saxon Society. I ask you?"

"When you spoke to your brother yesterday, did he say if he had any plans for the evening? Was he meeting anyone?"

"He didn't tell me, and I didn't ask. We had very little interest in each other's lives. He really was a very dull man." He stared at the body of his brother for a moment, wearing an expression Shadow couldn't read, before giving his head a brief shake.

"What about Mrs Underhill?"

Edmund's eyes narrowed a little. "What about her?"

"Was she here last night?" asked Shadow.

"No. I believe she went out for the evening and this

morning she went out for a ride as she does most mornings. She isn't back yet. She doesn't know about Kenelm. I tried calling her but the signal around here is terrible. Now, if you don't need me, I should return to my office."

With that he spun on his heel and marched back down the corridor.

"They do say grief can affect people in strange ways," said Sergeant Thornton diplomatically when he was out of earshot.

"Or not at all," murmured Shadow. "Let's go to speak to someone you said was upset. The housekeeper. Did you say her name was Kemp?"

"That's right, sir. Glenda Kemp. She's in the kitchen." He paused and frowned at the gate and the still-whimpering dog. "I don't want Badger barging his way in here and disturbing things. Should we open it or try to climb over?"

"Neither. We'll go back the way we came," replied Shadow who wasn't convinced that their unathletic companion would make it over the waist-high gate.

They retraced their steps through the garden and went round to the front of the house. Sergeant Thornton guided them through the front door and into what felt like a dark, wood-panelled labyrinth of corridors and passageways. Shadow realised they were getting close to the kitchen when he could hear the sound of sobbing.

CHAPTER TWO

Down 5 (8 letters)
Lug Barry along to break-in and take something that isn't his

AS SOON AS Shadow saw Glenda, he recognised her as the woman with the fixed smile in the photograph on the floor of Kenelm's study. She may have gained a few pounds and her dark hair may now be streaked with grey but otherwise she looked remarkably similar to her picture. Although, now she wasn't smiling. Her mouth was trembling as tears streamed down her face. She was sitting at the large pine table in the middle of the old-fashioned kitchen clutching a mug of tea. Sitting next to her was a large man in his fifties with dark hair and a neat moustache. He was making sympathetic noises as he patted Glenda's arm and looked like he was wished he was somewhere else. Shadow guessed he must be Trevor, the security guard, who was not related to Sergeant Thornton.

As soon as Sergeant Thornton introduced the two detectives from York, Glenda broke down sobbing violently, shaking her head and insisting, "It's all my fault."

"Why do you say that, Mrs Kemp?" asked Shadow, but

she was crying so loudly, he couldn't be sure she'd heard him. He turned to Trevor, whose eyes were fixed on two cut-glass tumblers sitting on the draining board.

"Did you give her a drink to calm her down?" he asked.

Trevor shook his head.

"They were here when I arrived," Glenda managed to stammer between sobs, "Kenelm must have had a visitor. I washed up before I left. I always like to leave the place neat and tidy for him." She broke down again.

Shadow motioned to Jimmy. "Bag them up, will you?" Then he turned to Trevor. "Perhaps we should speak to you first, Mr Thornton. Would you step outside for a moment, please? Sergeant Thornton, would you stay here with Mrs Kemp?"

"Good idea, Chief Inspector," agreed Sergeant Thornton. "I'll make you a fresh pot of tea, Glenda," he said loudly to the near-hysterical housekeeper as Trevor reluctantly followed Shadow and Jimmy out into corridor.

"Poor woman," said Jimmy before Shadow could open his mouth.

Trevor nodded. "She's taken it badly. She was very fond of Kenelm."

"Why does she think Kenelm's death is her fault?" asked Shadow.

"I couldn't get much sense out of her, but I reckon it's because of the gate for Badger. It was her idea, you see. Kenelm was worried Badger might damage this new map he'd found so Glenda suggested putting that gate up. They only put it up for him yesterday morning. I reckon she thinks if Badger was in the room with Kenelm, he'd have been able to protect him from whoever broke in. I'm not so sure of that myself. Badger might have barked but he's a big softie really."

"Did you hear him barking?" Trevor looked down at his feet and shook his head.

Shadow frowned and tried again. "What can you tell us about yesterday evening? I understand you are head of security here."

"That's right. I've worked here over twenty years and we've never had a break-in before."

"What time did you start work?"

"I got here at about five as usual. Most of the staff clock off at half past. Some of the delivery lads are a bit later, if they've been held up in traffic. I went around checking everything was locked up and the alarms were on like I always do. Edmund was still here in his office. He left at about six and Mrs Underhill left at about the same time."

"Did you see Kenelm Underhill?"

"Yes, at about half past six, I saw him through one of the mill windows. He was in the garden with Badger. I didn't speak to him just gave him a wave."

"Was Glenda still here then?"

"Yes, she cooks Kenelm his supper at about seven then goes home."

"I understand you left here at about ten o'clock. Don't you stay here all night?"

Trevor looked down again and shuffled his feet. "Most of the night, but sometimes I get a bit peckish so I nip home."

"Or to the pub," suggested Shadow repeating what Sergeant Thornton had told him.

"Well, I did last night, but not every night. I only had a pint then got some fish and chips and came straight back here. I couldn't have been gone more than half an hour," he floundered, looking even more uncomfortable. "Like I said, usually nothing ever happens."

"Until last night, when it looks like someone broke into your employer's home and killed him."

Trevor ran his hand through his hair. "Yes, I know. I know I should have been here," he admitted quietly. "It's not poor Glenda's fault. It's mine."

Shadow couldn't argue with him, but he didn't believe in kicking a man when he was down, so he changed tack. "You mentioned a new map Kenelm had," he said, recalling that Sergeant Thornton had also mentioned a precious document that Kenelm Underhill had wanted to keep his boisterous dog away from.

"That's right. Kenelm's latest obsession. He thought it would lead him to Alfred's Hoard."

Both detectives looked at him blankly.

"What's that?" asked Jimmy, his finger poised above his electronic notebook.

"Alfred's Hoard? It's some Saxon treasure that's meant to be buried around these parts. Hidden by King Alfred so the marauding Vikings couldn't get their hands on it, but then he went and got himself killed and nobody ever found it. Anyway, Kenelm and Lance have been trying to find this hoard since they were kids and last week Kenelm found an old map that he thought would lead him to it."

"And did it?" asked Jimmy.

"No. At least I don't think so. You don't think that was why they broke in, do you? Someone knew he'd found the treasure and wanted to steal it?"

"We're keeping an open mind at the moment, Mr Thornton," said Shadow, who personally thought the whole Saxon treasure story sounded quite fanciful.

"Are there any CCTV cameras on the premises, Mr Thornton?" asked Jimmy.

Trevor looked up and nodded. "Yes, we've got one at the main door to the mill and one in the courtyard, but none at the back of the house."

"We might still be able to see something."

"Yes, right. Do you want to come to my office and take a look?"

Jimmy looked at Shadow. "You go," he said. "I'll stay here and speak to Mrs Kemp. She might find it less overwhelming if there aren't two of us."

He waited a moment for Jimmy and Trevor to disappear through the back door, then returned to the kitchen. Sergeant Thornton was holding a large mug of tea and had his other hand in the biscuit barrel. His mouth was full of biscuit too. He mimed an offer of a cup of tea, but Shadow shook his head. Glenda Kemp was still in the same seat. She seemed to have calmed down but was still dabbing at her eyes and nose with a piece of scrunched-up kitchen roll. He sat down next to her.

"It must have been a terrible shock this morning. Are you up to talking about it?" he asked gently. Glenda nodded but didn't look at him. He waited silently as she took a deep breath.

"I didn't get here until nearly twelve," she began quietly. "Normally, I'm here at about eight, but I'd been to Whitby to do the weekly shop and run a few errands. I unpacked the shopping and, when I'd put everything away, I went to see what Kenelm would like for lunch. It was clear nobody had prepared any food since I tidied up last night, so I knew he hadn't had any breakfast, but that isn't so unusual when he's busy working on something. I don't think he even went to bed. He loses all track of time."

"What was he working on that was so important? This map showing Alfred's Hoard?"

Glenda looked up and nodded. "That's right. All his life he's wanted to find it. Everyone thought it was a myth. Then last week he found a map. It was really only a scrap of parchment but he was sure it would lead him to the treasure." She gave a small smile. "He was so excited."

"Where did he find this map?"

"It was in amongst some papers that belonged to his father. They were in a trunk in the attic."

"Did he tell many people about it?"

"Oh yes, everyone. As I said, he was very excited. He called a meeting of the Saxon Society."

"And when did you last see Mr Underhill?"

"It would have been a little after seven last night. I took him his supper on a tray to his study. It was a plain omelette and salad with a cup of tea and some shortbread for afterwards. He didn't have a big appetite and he preferred plain food."

"Mrs Underhill wasn't dining with her husband last night?"

Glenda looked down again. "No. She was going out for the evening. I saw her drive away at about six o'clock."

"And this morning. Can you tell me exactly what you saw?"

"I went down the corridor towards the study and knew something was wrong as soon as I saw Badger. He was sitting there so quiet. Normally he jumps up and wags his tail as soon as he sees me." Tears began to spill down her face again. "If only we hadn't put up that gate, he might have been able to protect Kenelm."

Shadow waited a moment for her to compose herself again and tried to ignore the crunching and slurping coming from the direction of Sergeant Thornton.

"Then when I looked through the doorway, I saw him," continued Glenda. "He was just lying there, and everything was such a mess and there was broken glass. I thought he must have fallen or had a stroke or a heart attack or something."

"Was he ill? Did he suffer from high blood pressure or heart disease?" asked Shadow thinking this was really a conversation he would have expected to have with Kenelm's wife.

Glenda shook her head slowly. "No, not exactly but he did suffer with his health. He often had dizzy spells and his stomach was a little weak."

"Had he seen his GP recently?"

"No. He preferred to use natural remedies when possible."

"Did you notice if anything from his study was missing?"

"No, I'm sorry, I didn't really look, and the place was such a mess. I knelt down and touched him. You know to see if he was…" She paused and swallowed. "He was so cold. I knew he was gone but I phoned 999 anyway. I didn't know what else to do."

"You did the right thing," Shadow reassured her. Out in the courtyard he could hear the sound of several cars arriving and a second later Jimmy put his head around the door.

"Sorry to interrupt, Chief, but Ben and Ollie and the others are here."

Shadow nodded and stood up. "Thank you very much

for your time, Mrs Kemp. I'll leave you with Sergeant Thornton who will take a statement from you." He glanced over to the local sergeant, who quickly swallowed and began brushing crumbs off his uniform. "I would appreciate it if you could stay here in case we need to ask you any further questions."

Glenda nodded silently and Shadow followed Jimmy out of the kitchen.

"Anything on the CCTV?" he asked as they tried to find their way back to the study.

"We had a quick spool through the images from last night, but nothing. I've asked Trevor to send me the recordings from the previous week. That's how far they go back. I thought whoever broke in might have, you know, cased the joint. Did Glenda say much?"

"It's strange. I thought it seemed quite obvious that a break-in had taken place and she did say she blamed herself for the dog being behind the gate. But her first thought when she saw Kenelm was that he'd died of natural causes. That he might have had some sort of turn or fit and broken the glass and fallen," he mused.

"Did she say anything else?" asked Jimmy.

"She confirmed what Sergeant Thornton and Trevor had already told us. Apparently, this map Kenelm was so excited about was found last week in some of his father's old papers. Any sign of Mrs Underhill yet?"

"Not yet. Do you want me to go to the stables and see if

I can find her?"

"No let's see what forensics and…" he paused "…hold on. If Sophie's up north, who's coming out to look at the body?"

"Donaldson. Sorry, Chief," replied Jimmy with a grimace.

Shadow shook his head. Dr Donaldson was one of his least favourite people.

"I wish he'd get on with retiring, like he keeps promising," he muttered as they followed the sound of loud woofing and arrived back at the gate into the study. The place was now swarming with people dressed in protective suits including Ben and Ollie the forensic scientists and Donaldson who was barking almost as loudly as Badger.

"Will someone shut that bloody dog up?" Then seeing Shadow: "I don't know how you expect me to work in these conditions. This is meant to be a crime scene not Crufts!"

"See if you can get him to calm down and go outside," said Shadow quietly to Jimmy.

"The dog or Donaldson?" joked Ollie who was kneeling by the gate and earnt himself a scowl.

"Try and tempt him with a treat?" suggested Ben, the other taller forensic scientist as he handed a tin of dog biscuits that had been on the desk over to Jimmy. "It's okay, I've checked it already for prints."

Holding Badger's collar with one hand and rattling the biscuit tin in the other, Jimmy attempted to coax the dog back down the corridor as Shadow struggled to open the child gate.

"I'll get that for you, Chief," offered Ollie helpfully, but as he flicked the catch and the gate swung open, Badger saw his chance. He broke free and dived through into the study, nearly knocking Shadow off his feet.

"For crying out loud," he grumbled as Jimmy leapt past him too. Badger dashed over to his master's body, barking and whining while Donaldson and Ben tried to fend him off.

"Badger, no! Here, boy," said a stern voice from the door into the garden. It was Alice Debenham. The dog immediately shut up and went to sit meekly by her feet.

"Miss Debenham you really shouldn't be here," said Shadow in exasperation.

"I'm sorry, Chief Inspector, but when Lance came to borrow my bike, he said he'd seen several police cars heading to the mill so I thought I would see if Kenelm was all right." She shook her head as she stared at the body. "Poor, poor man. May Badger and I have a moment alone with him?"

Shadow looked at her incredulously for a second before replying. "No, I'm afraid that won't be possible. Sergeant Chang, perhaps you would be kind enough to show Miss Debenham out." Then he lowered his voice. "And get one of those local officers to make sure nobody else gets into the garden," he hissed as Jimmy hurried over to escort Alice and Badger away from the crime scene.

"We may as well have stayed in York. You seem to have

brought the Shambles with you, Shadow," quipped Donaldson tutting and shaking his head as he inspected the body. "I shall be making a note of all this in my report. I'm struggling to remember a time when I was forced to work in a more disorganised environment."

"Well, they do say ageing affects the memory," replied Shadow testily. "Why don't you concentrate on telling me what you've discovered before there are any more interruptions."

Donaldson scowled but cleared his throat as was his habit before he made a proclamation. "Well, he was definitely murdered."

"The blow to the head?" asked Shadow.

"Certainly not. That would have hardly dazed him let alone kill him. He was stabbed and with some force. Look," he said gently rolling the body slightly to show an intricately carved bronze handle protruding from the victim's side.

"What's that? Some sort of knife?" he asked.

Donaldson gave him a superior look. "I believe it's a ceremonial dagger, probably an antique. I have a similar one, a *sgian dubh* for formal occasions," he replied, always keen to remind people of his Scottish heritage. "It looks to have entered the body between the third and fourth rib and probably went into his heart. There would have been a fair amount blood but as this carpet is red and thick pile, it may not have been immediately noticeable to whoever found him."

"So no chance it could have been an accident or a fall?" said Shadow almost to himself as he thought about what Glenda had said.

Donaldson snorted. "Hardly. Even if some freak stumble or fall had occurred, more force would have needed to be applied for the blade to enter the body as it did. No, whoever did this certainly meant it. It could of course have been self-inflicted but there's something else. He was partially strangled too." He pulled down the silk scarf to show a series of bruises around Kenelm's neck. Shadow frowned at the orderly pattern of purple and blue across the papery skin.

"They don't look like they were made by a human hand."

"No," agreed Donaldson slightly reluctantly. "My guess would be that dog's lead," he said pointing to the metal chain with the leather handle lying on the floor by the desk.

"Wow," said Jimmy who had joined them again. "Hit on the head, strangled, then stabbed. You make it sound like he was tortured or something."

Donaldson shrugged. "I won't be able to tell you any more until after the post-mortem. Until then, you can allow your imaginations to run wild," he said as he rose to his feet.

"What about time of death?" asked Shadow.

"I'd say between ten o'clock last night and one o'clock this morning. Do you know what time he had his evening meal?" he asked nodding towards the tray holding the broken, dirty plates and cutlery.

"It was an omelette at about seven o'clock."

"Good. As I said, I'll tell you more when I've opened him up."

Shadow nodded and turned his attention to Ben and Ollie.

"Have you two found anything yet?"

"Not yet, Chief," they replied in unison.

Shadow turned to Jimmy. "There's no point in us waiting here. Let's see if we can locate Mrs Underhill. I don't like the fact that nobody has been able to contact her. Glenda said nobody had prepared any food in the kitchen since last night. Are we sure she went out riding? There isn't a chance she's in the house somewhere, injured or worse?" he asked.

Jimmy frowned as he scrolled through his notes. "Erm, Sergeant Thornton said no other rooms had been disturbed and it was Edmund Underhill who said Mrs Underhill was out riding, and that he couldn't contact her on her phone. Nobody else has confirmed it."

"Utter shambles," muttered Donaldson again.

Shadow ignored him and beckoned for Jimmy to follow him out of the room. The two of them made their way back through the wood-panelled labyrinth.

"It's a creepy old place, isn't it, Chief? Even without a dead body," whispered Jimmy who was almost bent double beneath the low ceilings. Shadow ignored him. Unconvinced that Sergeant Thornton's search would have been particularly thorough, he was about to suggest they check the bedrooms, when from out in the courtyard, they heard the sound of horse's hooves.

"Hey, that could be her now," suggested Jimmy who never missed an opportunity to state the obvious.

When they found their way to the front door, they stepped outside and saw a woman leaving the stables that were outside the main entrance to the courtyard. As soon as she saw them, she came hurrying over. She was dressed in jodhpurs and a quilted jacket. Her dark hair was pulled back from her attractive face and secured with a large clip. Shadow guessed she was in her mid-forties. Before she reached them, Edmund Underhill suddenly appeared from the main entrance to the mill. The woman stopped when she saw him.

"Edmund, what's going on? What are the police doing here? And the ambulance?" she asked.

Edmund stepped forward and put a hand on her shoulder. "Olivia. It's Kenelm. He's dead. I tried to call you," Shadow heard him say as he and Jimmy hurried to join them.

"What do you mean dead? He can't be." The woman they now knew was definitely Kenelm's wife was shaking her head.

"It looks like someone broke into his study and killed him," continued Edmund. Then nodding to the two detectives. "This is Chief Inspector Shadow and Sergeant Chang."

"We're very sorry for your loss, Mrs Underhill. Are you up to answering some questions?" asked Shadow.

Olivia's eyes flicked over to Edmund, but she gave a brisk nod.

"Yes, I suppose so, yes."

"Would you like to go inside?"

"No. No, I'm fine here," she insisted.

"When did you last see your husband, Mrs Underhill?"

"At about six o'clock last night."

"I understand you went out yesterday evening."

"Yes, I was in Whitby."

"You didn't see your husband at all after that?"

"No. We keep very different hours. Kenelm was a night owl and I'm more of an early riser."

"Mrs Kemp said she didn't think Mr Underhill went to bed last night."

"She may well be right. She's far more au fait with Kenelm's routine than I am." There was a slight edge in her voice. "You may as well know, if Glenda hasn't told you already, my husband and I had separate bedrooms."

"Do the two of you have any children?"

"We have a son, Cedric," she said, then noticing the re-action on Jimmy's face: "He goes by Ric, Sergeant. It could have been worse. Kenelm wanted to call him Beowulf. He's twenty-three now and a bond trader in New York." She glanced at her watch. "I won't bother him until the markets close over there."

"Mrs Kemp mentioned a map that your husband had recently found," said Shadow.

Olivia rolled her eyes. "That stupid map! It was barely that—more a scrap of old paper or parchment or whatever he called it. He's been searching for that Saxon treasure for as long as I've known him. It probably doesn't even exist. This map was his latest obsession, Chief Inspector. Before that he and Alice thought they might find it using ley lines or some other nonsense."

"It looks like there may have been a break-in. Have either you or your husband been worried about intruders? I notice you don't have an alarm."

"No. Our insurance company kept telling us to install one and it would certainly have reduced our premiums, but Kenelm wouldn't hear of it. The engineers might have damaged his precious house you see. Honestly, it's a miracle he allowed us to have running water and electricity."

"You haven't seen anybody suspicious hanging around? Somebody who caught your attention. Somebody you didn't recognise," continued Shadow.

"In Ellerdale? No, Chief Inspector. It's always the same old faces hanging around here." He noted the edge in her voice again.

"Can you think of anyone who may have wanted to harm your husband?" he asked. She shook her head slowly and glanced over to Edmund Underhill.

"No, Chief Inspector, nobody," she said. Producing a handkerchief from her pocket, she began to dab at her eyes, but Shadow couldn't see any tears.

Edmund Underhill stepped forward. "I think that's enough for now, Chief Inspector. Olivia has had quite a shock. We both have. Come along, Liv, I'll take you inside and fix you a stiff drink."

With that he put his arm around her shoulder and guided her inside the house. The two detectives watched them in silence until the front door was closed firmly behind them.

Jimmy exhaled loudly. "Wow. Neither of them seemed very upset, did they, Chief?"

"No," agreed Shadow. "But perhaps Sergeant Thornton is right, and grief affects people differently. I thought it was strange that neither of them asked how he was killed though. That's usually the first thing they want to know. Let's go back to the village and see what the locals are saying. Then we'll collect the car and return to York. I doubt Donaldson or forensics will have anything else to tell us until tomorrow."

They retraced the route they had taken along the beck. As they did, Shadow noticed a small jetty at the bottom of the garden where there was a wooden rowing boat tied up. He couldn't recall noticing it before. He was about to mention it to Jimmy, but his sergeant had already launched into his latest theory.

"I was thinking about this treasure Kenelm was looking for. What if he had already found it and somebody wanted to steal it from him? There could be a gang targeting rural villages like this or one that specialises in stealing ancient artefacts or something. I could get in touch with the NCA and check with them."

"You do that," said Shadow but he was less interested in what the National Crime Agency may or may not deign to share with them and keener to learn about the inhabitants of Ellerdale. "What happened to Badger?" he asked.

"Alice Debenham took him through the garden and round to the kitchen to keep Glenda company. She seemed to know her way around the place. She said she'd take him through the back door, so I left her to it. Why?"

"He was barking his head off when the place was full of strangers, but he shut up as soon as Alice told him to."

"Maybe she's just good with animals."

"Or perhaps Kenelm knew whoever attacked him, which is why Badger didn't bark."

"Or maybe he did bark but it was when Trevor was in the pub so nobody heard him."

Shadow nodded. His sergeant had a point. According to the time of death Donaldson had given, the security guard's timing had been terrible or perfect depending on which way you looked at it.

"Make sure you look into Trevor's background and everyone else who works at the mill," he said.

"Will do, Chief. I'll check if anyone's been sacked recently too. You know, in case they bear a grudge or something."

As they followed the path past the back of the church, Jimmy nudged him with his elbow. "Chief, I think someone is trying to get our attention," he said pointing to the churchyard.

The vicar was hurrying down the path towards them and waving frantically. He was about Shadow's age. A small, wiry man with neatly trimmed dark hair and beard.

"Are you the police?" he asked as he drew level with them.

"Yes, sir. I'm Chief Inspector Shadow and this Detective Sergeant Chang."

The vicar shook both their hands.

"I'm Tristram Prescott, the vicar here at St Cuthbert's. What on earth is going on? I've seen and heard at least half a dozen emergency vehicles racing through the village. While I sympathise with Lance having his house broken into, isn't all this activity a bit of an overreaction?"

"I'm sorry to have to tell you, Reverend, that as well as the burglary, we are also investigating the death of one of your parishioners: Dr Kenelm Underhill," explained Shadow.

The vicar's hand flew to his face. "Oh dear me, what a dreadful thing to happen. Poor Kenelm. He always suffered with his health. I shall pray for him of course." He shook his head. "And he was such a valued member of the committee too. I don't know if you are aware, Chief Inspector, but we are expecting the judges to arrive any day now. Kenelm was going to help me show them around."

Shadow frowned as he tried to recall what Natalie had

said. Wasn't it Reverend Prescott who had objected to the police tape down at Camelot Cottage?

"The judges for the best kept village?" he enquired.

"England's Perfect Village," corrected the vicar. "There will be stiff competition from Grassington, Thornton le Dale and Hovingham, but we are very hopeful. The others are all beautiful villages in their own way, but they don't have our secret weapon," he said proudly gesturing to the church behind him.

"It's really pretty," said Jimmy.

"Oh it's not simply pretty, Sergeant. St Cuthbert's is one of the few remaining Anglo-Saxon churches in the country. Parts of it date back to 850AD."

"Are you having problems with the roof?" asked Shadow who had spotted some scaffolding poles poking out from behind the far side wall.

Reverend Prescott looked perturbed. "Oh, I was rather hoping you couldn't see that nasty but necessary intrusion from the twenty-first century. I certainly don't want the judges to think it detracts from the beauty of the church. Naturally, with a building of this age, maintenance never ends but the cost of a new roof has been quoted as almost three hundred thousand pounds. We have set up an appeal and I was very much hoping winning this competition would generate some much-needed publicity."

Shadow decided to leave him to fret in peace.

"I hope the judging goes well, Reverend," he began as he

attempted to move away.

"Oh, there is one more thing, Chief Inspector. I want to report an incident of vandalism. Someone has tried digging up our sundial."

Shadow and Jimmy exchanged a glance as Reverend Prescott beckoned them over to a square stone pillar about halfway up the path to the church. With a sigh, Shadow dutifully made his way over to the area of ground Reverend Prescott was pointing to. He knelt down to take a closer look. On each side of the sundial's pillar four identically sized squares of turf had been cut out and replaced. The side of each square was about six inches in length. Shadow lifted one square up. There was only bare soil beneath.

"It happened sometime after eight o'clock yesterday evening, but I didn't discover it until almost midnight. It's an extremely old and rare sundial. Anglo-Saxon of course, like the church itself. Do you think someone was trying to steal it?" asked the vicar.

"They didn't try very hard if they were," replied Shadow. The pillar itself didn't look to have been touched. "Also as it's extremely rare it would be very difficult for a thief to sell on."

Shadow studied the top of the pillar. Instead of the brass or bronze circular plaque he was expecting, the 'dial' had been carved into the stone itself. It was a semicircle surrounded by various runic symbols.

Reverend Prescott shook his head solemnly. "I hate to

cast aspersions, but do you think it could be someone trying to sabotage our chances?"

"You think someone from one of the other villages might be responsible?" asked Jimmy, who had been busy taking photographs and notes, despite Shadow's scepticism.

"It's no secret that Ellerdale is the favourite to win, Sergeant. I stayed here on guard to ensure they didn't try and strike again."

"You were here all night?" asked Jimmy.

"Yes, until daybreak. Then Trevor, who saw me on his way home, was kind enough to step in, so I could go for a shower, but then he was called away to Mill House. Now I understand why."

"Did you see or hear anything unusual while you were here?" asked Shadow.

"No, not really. Although I did think I heard a couple of loud splashes in the early hours, but assumed it was an animal of some sort." He hesitated. "I admit I may have dozed off for a short while, but I sat with my back against the sundial, so if the vandals returned, they would wake me. I am still concerned whoever did this may strike again."

"We'll look into it. Thank you, Reverend," said Shadow firmly turning to go and determined to leave this time.

"Do you think you could post a guard by the gate? Ideally, a non-uniform officer. As I said before I don't want to draw attention to the fact our beloved church may be a crime scene," Tristram called after him.

"I don't think that will be possible, Reverend. As I'm sure you understand our officers are a little overstretched at the moment," he replied without stopping.

"Oh dear, then we shall have to organise a rota of willing volunteers," Shadow heard him murmur as they stepped through the gate and continued on their way.

"He never asked how Dr Underhill had died either," said Jimmy as soon as they were out of earshot. "And he didn't seem that bothered."

"He seemed more upset about his roof and his sundial than the fact that one of his flock has been killed," agreed Shadow. "And like Glenda, he assumed it was natural causes. She said he didn't visit the doctor very often but see if you can find out who his GP was."

"The sundial thing is a bit weird though," continued Jimmy as he tapped away at his notebook. "Like Natalie said, nothing happens here then a break-in, a murder and some vandalism in the church. Can it really be coincidence?"

"Trouble comes in threes," muttered Shadow. "It isn't the only coincidence. What are the chances of someone digging up this churchyard on the same night someone was in Museum Gardens."

Jimmy looked surprised. "There's over twenty miles between here and York. Do you really think there's a connection? I assumed it was kids messing about. Do you think it could be metal detectorists striking again?"

"I don't know. It seems a bit odd, that's all."

After a few more minutes they had found their way back to Camelot Cottage. Jimmy was busy fielding calls while Shadow trudged alongside deep in thought, trying to make sense of all the information that had been slung at him in the last few hours. They were walking round to the front of the cottage, when Natalie came hurrying towards them.

"Everything all right, sir?" she asked eagerly.

"Not really. Not only do we have a murder on our hands, but we still have this burglary and now a case of vandalism at the church to deal with," he replied irritably. He hated been interrupted when he was thinking, and he'd never liked being called sir. It reminded him of his time at boarding school where all the masters seemed to have a sadistic streak.

"Dr Underhill's death wasn't an accident then?" she asked quietly, looking suitably chastised.

"We don't think so," explained Jimmy giving her a sympathetic smile. "But we aren't making any details public yet."

"Of course, Sergeant," she agreed quickly.

"Is Mr Debenham still here?" asked Shadow. He was interested to see his reaction to his friend's death.

"No. He wanted to go into Whitby but there aren't any buses so he said he'd go and borrow a bike from his sister. He bought her one of those folding ones for Christmas apparently."

Shadow gave a brisk nod. "Will you ask him to contact us when he returns?"

"Yes, sir. You said something had happened at the church?" she asked.

"It looks like someone has tried to dig up the sundial," replied Jimmy.

Natalie frowned. "That must have been the incident Reverend Prescott mentioned to Sergeant Thornton this morning. He wanted us to go and take a look, but we were too busy here. Are you sure it was a person? Could it be a badger?"

"Kenelm Underhill's dog?" asked Shadow who had only been half listening.

"No, sir," she replied. "There's a badger sett not far from here. You can sometimes see where they've been digging in the woods next to the beck."

"Really? I've never seen a badger before," replied Jimmy.

Shadow raised his eyes to the sky. The last time the two of them were investigating a crime in the countryside, his sergeant had carried a wildlife book with him. Ticking off any birds or animals he encountered. It had nearly driven Shadow mad, but Natalie was beaming at him.

"I'm a volunteer with a local wildlife group. We've set up a hide in the top of the woods with a motion-detection camera and everything. You know so we can keep an eye on them. We don't want to disturb them, so we keep their whereabouts quiet, but I'll take you up there sometime." Then she saw Shadow's face. "You know, when you aren't so busy…" She trailed off.

"I'd love that," agreed Jimmy enthusiastically. "It would be great if I could bring my wife too. She knows loads about animals. She grew up on a farm."

"Sure," she replied.

"Yes, yes, very interesting," interrupted Shadow, "but unless these badgers have square paws, they aren't our churchyard vandals."

Natalie looked crestfallen once more and from the corner of his eye, he saw Jimmy mouth 'sorry' to her. He followed the garden path, to the front of the cottage, with Natalie and Jimmy behind. Shadow pointed to the market square where he could see at least three public houses.

"Which of the pubs is the best for local gossip?" he asked.

"The Black Bull," replied Natalie immediately, picking out a large square Georgian building that Shadow guessed had once been a coaching inn.

"Good." Shadow turned to Jimmy. "We'll see what the locals have to say about what's been going on." Then to the young community support officer: "Are you all right staying here? I don't know when the CSI team will make it down, but I assume your sergeant will send someone to relieve you soon."

"Yes, sir," she replied meekly.

"Thanks for all your help today, Natalie. We really appreciate it," added Jimmy as Shadow strode away. Not for the first time, he considered his sergeant may have been better suited to life in the diplomatic service.

CHAPTER THREE

Down 2 (10 letters)
Germanic settlers were lax when they sang at noon

THE TWO DETECTIVES crossed the road carefully as the sheep who had escaped earlier had left plenty of evidence behind. As they approached the Black Bull, Shadow noticed a terrace of neat houses. They looked like they had been built after the war and the sign in front of them read *Underhill Row*.

"That must be where Glenda Kemp lives," he said.

Jimmy checked his notes. "That's right. Number two. The one in the middle. The Underhills must have been here a long time. Even the street is named after them."

"Lance Debenham said his family used to own the whole village. I wonder when the Underhills became the more prominent family," pondered Shadow.

Jimmy grinned. "I bet he's miffed there isn't a street named after his family."

They entered the pub. It was extremely busy for a Tuesday afternoon. Various groups of men and women were huddled around the tables chatting quietly. The atmosphere seemed subdued, concerned even. Shadow guessed they must be the workers from Underhill's Mill who had been sent home early. A young man was standing at the bar. He was tall and broad with dark hair and a few days' growth of stubble on his face. Shadow watched him drain his pint and slam it down on the bar.

"Same again, Mick."

"Steady on, Kempy. This'll be your fourth," replied the grey-haired, red-faced barman.

"Who are you, my mother? Besides I'm in mourning," he said with a grin.

"Excuse me," said Shadow as he approached the young man. "Are you related to Glenda Kemp?"

The man looked him up and down and scowled. "Who wants to know?"

"I'm Chief Inspector Shadow and this is Detective Sergeant Chang."

The young man sneered. "You didn't waste any time, did you? Forget that pint, Mick. I'll be going. Your clientele has gone right downhill."

"Sorry about him, gentlemen. He's had a few," apologised the barman as the young man stomped out, barging into two other customers as he went.

"Who is he?" asked Shadow.

"Craig Kemp and yes, he is Glenda's son. He's not a bad lad, just a bit mouthy especially when he's had a few. Speaking of which, what can I get you gentlemen?"

"I'll have a pint of Theakston's and…" He turned to Jimmy.

"A mineral water for me please, Chief."

"Mr Kemp said he was in mourning?" continued Shadow as the barman began to pull a pint.

"His idea of a joke. He's a delivery driver for Underhills. Half the workforce have been in here since they heard." He frowned as he placed their drinks on the bar. "Isn't that why you're here? About Kenelm, I mean, or is it the break-in at Lance's place?"

"We are investigating both incidents," replied Shadow as he took a sip of his pint.

The barman leant across the bar and lowered his voice. "I heard there was a break-in at Mill House too. Do you reckon they're connected? Only our alarm is on the blink. Should I get it fixed?"

"Better to be safe than sorry," Shadow whispered back as he wondered if there was a village that took security less seriously than Ellerdale. "Was Trevor Thornton, the security guard from Underhills, in here last night?" he asked.

The barman looked at them both a little apprehensively before nodding.

"Yes, Trev arrived at about half ten, I think. He didn't stay long though."

"Was Mrs Kemp in here too?" he asked.

The barman shook his head. "No, not Glenda. Craig was though, along with half the village. Monday is our quiz night. It's very popular. We were packed."

"Did you notice anything unusual last night? Any strangers in the village?"

"Not really. As I said we were busy. We get teams coming from other villages for the quiz, but nobody I hadn't seen before."

"Did Dr Underhill drink in here often?"

"Kenelm? No, he wasn't the sociable type but his brother, Edmund, often stops in for a quick drink after work. Nice bloke. Calls a spade a spade mind you and doesn't suffer fools but not too up himself even if he is an Underhill. Happy to buy a round and always puts some money behind the bar for the Christmas party. You know the type."

Shadow nodded even though it didn't sound much like the rather cold and aloof man he'd met.

The barman looked thoughtful for a second. "Come to think of it Kenelm did used to come here a bit. He would hire the back room for a meeting of his Saxon Society. Once a month I think it was. He'd order food and drinks but I'm going back a few years now. Before his dad died. Excuse me will you, gentlemen."

He disappeared to the other side of the bar to serve another customer while Shadow and Jimmy took their drinks over to a table by the window overlooking the marketplace.

"Who are these Saxons that people keep going on about, Chief?" asked Jimmy.

"Did you attend any history lessons at school, Sergeant?"

replied Shadow wearily.

Jimmy shrugged. "We did the Romans and the war and stuff, but we didn't cover it all."

"The Saxons, sometimes called the Anglo-Saxons, ruled England from roughly the time the Romans left to when the Normans invaded, although sometimes their kingdoms overlapped with the Vikings especially in this part of the country."

Jimmy didn't look particularly enlightened. "So, time wise?" he asked.

Shadow sighed. "Around 500 to 1066." Then as an after-thought: "AD."

"Okay, got it. Although technically you should say CE not AD."

"What?"

"It's a new thing. CE not AD and BCE not BC. It means Common Era and Before Common Era."

"Why on earth do they have to meddle with things all the time?" tutted Shadow, taking another drink of his pint.

"I think it's to make things simpler, Chief."

"For whom? We've been using AD and BC for centu-ries."

Jimmy didn't bother to reply; instead his face clouded as he checked his phone.

"Anything wrong?" asked Shadow.

"No, just a text from Sophie telling me she's turning off her phone for a bit. She's going to see her dad in hospital and is hoping they'll discharge him so he can go home later today."

They sat in silence for a moment, then Shadow spotted Alice Debenham wafting her way across the marketplace.

"When she was up at Mill House did you get the impression that she knew Kenelm was dead when she arrived?" he asked.

Jimmy looked thoughtful for a few seconds then shook his head. "Not really. I think it was like she said. She and Lance heard all the police cars, and she came to see what was going on," he replied.

Shadow nodded and downed the last of his pint. "Come on. It's time we headed back to York."

They left the pub and crossed the square back to Camelot Cottage where their car was still parked outside. However, as they were about to climb in, Lance Debenham appeared at the front gate carrying the folded bicycle.

"Hello, Mr Debenham. How's Merlin?" asked Jimmy.

"He still seems rather unsettled, Sergeant, but the vet can't see him until this evening. Is it true that Kenelm is dead? Alice left me a rather garbled message when I was in Whitby at the insurers, but now she isn't answering her phone and Natalie wouldn't tell me anything either."

"Yes, I'm afraid it is true," said Shadow. "I'm sorry. I understand he was a friend of yours."

Lance stared blankly at him before slowly nodding his head. "Yes, we've been best friends since we were children.

What happened?"

"We're still investigating the incident," replied Shadow.

"Incident? Forgive me, Chief Inspector, but that doesn't sound like he died from natural causes."

"Would you have expected him to? Was he ill?"

"No, at least not seriously. But he wasn't what you would call robust. He was always complaining about some ailment or other. I'm afraid I didn't take him very seriously. Should I have done?"

"We are awaiting the results of the post-mortem but we don't believe he died of natural causes. We think he may have been killed during an attempted burglary."

"Somebody broke into Mill House last night too? Good Lord, what is the world coming to? If only Badger could have protected him. Is that why nobody has been down here to take fingerprints or whatever? Natalie told me I can't start tidying up yet."

"We appreciate your cooperation, Mr Debenham, and apologise for the delay. The crime scene and forensics should be with you by the end of the day," explained Jimmy.

Shadow watched Lance closely. Although he had expressed more concern than either Kenelm's brother or wife, for a man who had lost his best friend, he seemed very composed and something he'd said jarred in his head.

"When did you last see, Dr Underhill?" he asked.

"I went to see him briefly on Friday morning before I left."

"Can you think of any reason why your home and Mill House may have been targeted, Mr Debenham?" he asked.

"No," replied Lance, "I assumed they broke in here because they knew nobody was at home."

"I understand Mr Underhill shared your interest in Saxon history," said Shadow.

Lance nodded his head vigorously. "Yes indeed, Chief Inspector, since we were boys. He and I formed the Ellerdale Saxon Society over thirty years ago."

"Are there many members?" asked Jimmy, his finger poised over his electronic notebook.

"Kenelm was the chair, I was the treasurer, Glenda acted as secretary. Alice attended meetings when she felt like it. Other members came and went over the years, but we were the stalwarts. We met once month, via Zoom during term for my benefit. Oh, I almost forgot Tristram. He's also a member and our local vicar."

"Yes, we've already met Reverend Prescott," said Shadow.

"He told us someone was trying to dig up the sundial last night too," added Jimmy, earning himself a scowl from Shadow.

Lance looked surprised. "Really how very strange." He paused. "Is there any chance it could have been Kenelm?"

"Why do you think it might be him?" asked Shadow.

"Last week, Kenelm asked Tristram for permission to excavate a small area of land surrounding the sundial.

Tristram told him he would need to get permission from the archbishop's office. Personally, I think Tristram was just stalling Kenelm. He didn't want his churchyard looking a mess before the judges turned up. No doubt you have heard about the England's Perfect Village competition. Tristram is very keen Ellerdale wins."

"Was Kenelm's request connected to the map he had found recently? Glenda Kemp mentioned it," asked Shadow, wondering why the vicar hadn't mentioned Kenelm wanting to dig in the churchyard.

"Yes, indeed, a very exciting discovery and Kenelm was convinced it would lead him to Alfred's Hoard. He called a special meeting of the Saxon Society last Thursday. However, Tristram insisted he would need proof that the map was genuine before seeking permission. Kenelm said he would consider taking it to the experts in York, but he was never a very patient man."

"He thought the treasure, the hoard was buried in the churchyard?"

"He thought it was a possible location. I didn't agree. You must understand the map was very old and not easy to either read or interpret."

"Did you actually see this map?"

Lance hesitated. "Only once, very briefly, Chief Inspector. Kenelm was very protective of it. He never did like to share."

"And when was this?"

"Last Thursday evening, Chief Inspector, at the meeting of the Saxon Society."

"Where was this meeting held?"

"At the Mill House. In Kenelm's study."

"Can you give us a description at all?" asked Jimmy. Lance looked slightly irritated as he had when they'd first spoken to him.

"I can't imagine you will stumble over many other maps from the Saxon era to confuse it with, Sergeant," he replied. "From what I can remember it was in fact two pieces of parchment: one showing a very rudimental plan, on the other was some writing."

"What did it say?"

"That's what Kenelm was trying to decipher," replied Lance impatiently.

"Was it in Latin?" asked Shadow.

"If only, Chief Inspector. It was in Old English—far more difficult to read."

"And this map was meant to show the location of some treasure?" asked Jimmy again as he noted everything down.

"Yes, Sergeant. Alfred's Hoard as it has come to be known." Then seeing Jimmy's blank expression. "Do I take it your knowledge is somewhat lacking when it comes to the Saxons, Sergeant?"

"They came after the Romans and before the Normans," replied Jimmy parroting the information he'd just learnt. "Was King Alfred running away from the Romans when he buried this treasure that's meant to be on the map?" he asked.

Lance's face broke into an indulgent smile. "Come inside and I shall explain all. Luckily whoever broke in left my library untouched."

"This had better not be a waste of time," muttered Shadow as they followed Lance into the cottage and through a door next to the front door that Shadow had assumed was a cloakroom.

"My sanctuary," declared Lance grandly. It turned out his library was little more than a large cupboard lined with shelves. Shadow and Jimmy squeezed themselves on to the narrow window seat while Lance perched on the edge of the small armchair, adjusted his glasses, leant forward and cleared his throat. Shadow imagined it was a pose he had struck a thousand times before in front of his classes at the prep school.

"Now, gentlemen," he began, "I expect you are thinking King Alfred of the burning cakes."

Shadow could see Jimmy open his mouth and quickly nudged him in the ribs to shut him up. Although it might be worth their while finding out about this supposed treasure, they certainly didn't have time to fill in all the gaps in Jimmy's historical knowledge stretching back over the last fifteen hundred years. "In fact," continued Lance, "you would be wrong. That Alfred who has come to be known as the Great, ruled Mercia about one hundred and fifty after our Alfred, who should more correctly be called Aldfrith. Aldfrith was king of Northumbria from about 685 to 705."

"My wife's from Northumbria," interjected Jimmy.

Lance gave another indulgent smile and Shadow was half expecting him to pat his sergeant on the head. It seemed his instincts about Mr Debenham had been correct. He was far happier when he was in control of the conversation.

"At that time, the Kingdom of Northumbria consisted of Bernicia and Deira. Bernicia was the area that we now call Northumberland with Hexham and Bamburgh being important sites, whereas Deira was a large part of what we now know as North Yorkshire with York, Whitby and Ripon the main commercial and religious centres. Although Northumbria flourished under Aldfrith's rule, it was still the target of Viking raiders. One of these raids on Whitby took place when Aldfrith was there. Unprepared for such an attack, he and his followers fled inland via the River Esk, which our beck runs into. Knowing they were outnumbered, Aldfrith and his men buried the most valuable items they were carrying before the inevitable battle. Sadly, Aldfrith did not survive long enough to retrieve his treasure, as he and almost all his followers were killed by the Viking raiders not far from here. They are said to have been buried near the treasure and near the beck. In fact, the beck is still called the Bloody Beck after it ran red with the blood of the slain Saxons. It's very much part of local legend. Kenelm and I have been looking for the site of both the burial ground and the treasure ever since we first heard this story from our fathers."

"You were hoping to find a northern Sutton Hoo?" asked Shadow.

Lance's face fell a little. "Well, perhaps not so grand as that, Chief Inspector. I expect the bodies of Aldfrith and the others would have been buried quickly without much ceremony. However, at the very least we hoped to find coins, weapons of equal quality to the Gilling sword found not far from here in the 1970s and if we were very lucky some jewellery too, maybe even a crown." His eyes were almost glazing over at the thought of it.

"Even if that were the case, is it realistic to think it would still be recognisable as such after being buried all these years?" asked Shadow, who was thinking the local soil was very different to that down in Suffolk.

Lance snapped back to reality and looked offended. "I see no reason why not. After all, the Ryedale Hoard was extremely well persevered and was over eighteen hundred years old."

"Was Aldfrith related to King Arthur?" asked Jimmy as Merlin the cat sauntered into the room.

Lance chuckled again. "King Arthur and the Arthurian legends are just that, Sergeant. A myth. Albeit a myth my family have embraced. Now give me a moment and I shall explain exactly where Aldfrith fits in on the timeline of Saxon kings."

Lance retrieved several books then proceeded to lecture them on the lineage of Saxon kings and how the country had been divided. He was clearly passionate about the subject and had a willing audience in Jimmy. Shadow was more preoccupied with thoughts of the investigation. If Lance was correct and Camelot Cottage had been targeted because he was away, why hadn't the thieves struck at the empty holiday cottage next door but one? And why hadn't the intruders touched this library when they had made such a mess elsewhere in the cottage? Surely they would have knocked at least a few books off the shelves in the hope of finding something valuable hidden there. Did they ignore it because they thought it was a cupboard? Or was it possible they had been disturbed? Perhaps by people leaving the pub at closing time. He peered out of the window. There was a clear view across the square. In fact, the fish and chip shop was almost directly opposite. It would have been easy for anyone in the cottage standing by this window or the one in the sitting room to see Trevor getting his supper. If they were local, they would know he was the security guard at Underhill's Mill. Is that why they left Camelot Cottage and went up to Mill House, hoping it would be a more lucrative target? A local would also have known that Lance had gone away and that this place would be empty too.

Shadow's thoughts were interrupted by Jimmy.

"Did you know that, Chief? Athelstan was the first An-glo-Saxon king to rule the whole of England. He was the son of Edward the Elder and Egg, Egg…"

"Ecgwynn," supplied Lance. "Yes indeed, in my opinion it was Athelstan who should be known as the Great. A brave warrior and a pious man too. In fact, it was Athelstan who founded our church here in Ellerdale. Sadly, the Vikings retook this area of the country after his death, but we eventually got it back again."

"Yes, it's very interesting," agreed Shadow rising to his feet, "but we should be going. Thank you for your time, Mr Debenham, and once again please accept our condolences."

"One moment, Chief Inspector. I have some books here that I am sure will help you with your official inquiries," said Lance as he climbed a rickety ladder to retrieve several books from the highest shelves.

"Oh, I should also inform you that I will be returning to Durham on the next train from Whitby to collect my bike, but I shall return home again by tonight should you need me."

"You aren't continuing with your holiday?" asked Jimmy.

Lance shook his head solemnly. "I really don't think it would be appropriate under the circumstances, Sergeant."

Half an hour after entering the cottage, they finally escaped back to the car although Jimmy was laden down with the books Lance insisted he took home to read.

"I don't think I'm ever going to get through all these, Chief. I can't even pronounce half the names; Oswiu,

Ecgfrith, Ceolwulf," he said stumbling over the words as he flicked through the books before placing them on the back seat. "I might see if there's something on YouTube I can watch instead."

"Or instead, you could check and see if there are any updates on our current investigation. Your mobile has been suspiciously quiet."

Jimmy fished his phone out of his pocket and pulled a face. "Sorry, Chief, I'd switched it off by mistake when I read Sophie's text."

"For crying out loud," grumbled Shadow. He knew talking to Lance had been a waste of time. Jimmy could have googled what the Alfred Hoard was. His sergeant was now busy scrolling. "But we haven't missed much," he said. "Kenelm's body has been taken away and there's a message from Ben. Olivia, Glenda and Alice all had a look in the study after he and the forensics team had finished to see if they could identify what, if anything, had been taken. In brackets he's put 'Awks'."

"What's that?"

"It means awkward."

"Why was it awkward?"

"I don't know. He doesn't say, Chief."

Shadow tutted again. Only a member of his forensics team could manage to irritate him via a relayed text message.

"But," continued Jimmy, "it turns out the only things missing from the study were a bottle of Alice's rhubarb gin, some cash from his wallet, about fifty quid at the most probably. He didn't have any bank cards apparently. Three small pieces of Anglo-Saxon metalwork that were kept on his desk and antique ceremonial dagger from the tenth century that he used as a letter opener. We're assuming that was the murder weapon."

"Was the metalwork valuable?"

"Erm, they don't say." Jimmy continued to scroll. "They were made of bronze. Bronze isn't that valuable, is it?"

"Two break-ins and one dead body for what? Added together, the items they took must only be worth a few hundred quid at most."

"Maybe it was a junkie looking for cash for a quick fix."

"Round here? I can't see it," replied Shadow shaking his head. "And even if that were the case, they would be more likely to find cash in the pub's till or even at the chip shop."

"Then it must be this old treasure map everyone is going on about. Maybe it's really valuable. Everyone say's Kenelm was pretty excited about it."

"But was it even genuine? And if it was what they were after, why target Lance's cottage too?" asked Shadow.

"Remember what Lance said about Kenelm wanting to dig up near the sundial. Do you think he could have snuck into the churchyard at night, found the treasure and then someone, who must have been watching him, killed him for it? That would make more sense than murdering someone for some booze and a bit of cash."

Shadow frowned. As far as he could see nothing was making sense.

"Get Tom to run a background check on anyone in the village connected to Kenelm," he said.

Jimmy's phone pinged.

"It's another message from Ben. They thought the map was missing too along with Kenelm's notebook, but Glenda has told them that Kenelm took the map to some expert in York on Friday afternoon. She couldn't remember their name but it's the woman who is in charge of the Saxon Society there."

"Find out who she is," he instructed.

Jimmy obediently began tapping away on this phone and after a few seconds a smile of recognition appeared on his face. "Hey! It's Dr Shepherd."

"Who?" asked Shadow who was still thinking about the sundial at the church.

"You remember. Dr Dorothy Shepherd. She's in charge of the Roman Museum. We met her when those coins had been stolen from there."

Shadow nodded as details of that particular case slowly came back to him. He checked his watch.

"If you put your foot down. We might catch her before the museum closes."

"Great. Let's go!"

Shadow immediately regretted his words as Jimmy revved the engine and spun the wheels on the way out of the village.

"I said put your foot down not turn into Fangio," he complained through clenched teeth.

"Who?"

"Never mind. Just look where you're going."

"By the way, what's Sutton Hoo, the Gilling sword and the Ryedale Hoard? I was going to ask but I know you don't like getting sidetracked, Chief."

"Finally, the penny has dropped," muttered Shadow digging his fingernails into his seat belt as Jimmy swerved to avoid a pheasant. "Sutton Hoo is a large Anglo-Saxon burial site that included a ship and was found in East Anglia in the 1930s. The Gilling sword was, as the name suggests, a Saxon sword found not far from here at Gilling, by a schoolboy in the 1970s."

"Lucky kid! Did he get to keep it?"

"No, but I think he got a Blue Peter badge. And the Ryedale Hoard was a collection of Roman bronzes found near Ampleforth by metal detectorists."

"Wow! And we're back to the metal detectorists again."

Shadow nodded but he was thinking about Kenelm. The three people who were closest to him: his brother, wife and best friend had each reacted as if his death meant very little to them. Only his housekeeper had appeared grief-stricken. Did that tell him something about them or about the dead man? Despite Jimmy's talk of drug addicts and professional criminal gangs, he had the distinct feeling that Kenelm was killed by someone who knew him.

He wasn't sure how his nerves or his fingernails had survived when they finally screeched to a halt in the car park of Eboracum, York's museum dedicated to Roman history. Dr Shepherd, the museum's director, looked pleased to see them when her secretary showed Shadow and Jimmy into her office.

"Chief Inspector, Sergeant Chang, what a nice surprise," she said.

"Thank you for seeing us, Dr Shepherd. I'm sorry it's so late and we didn't make an appointment."

"Not at all, not at all. Now do take and seat. Thank you, Brian, no need to wait. I'll show the gentlemen out."

The secretary quickly disappeared as Shadow and Jimmy sat down in the two chairs Dr Shepherd had ushered them towards.

"I understand you are the chair of York's Saxon Society, Dr Shepherd," began Shadow.

"Yes, for my sins, Chief Inspector. It's not really my area of interest, but the university's Saxon expert is currently on sabbatical over in Germany, and as I still lecture at the university too, I offered to stand in. There's only about fifty or so members, mainly history and archaeology students from the university and we only meet once a month, so it's not too onerous. May I ask why you want to know?"

"Did a Dr Underhill of Ellerdale come to you with a map he'd found recently?"

"Kenelm? Yes. He came to see me on Friday. He seemed quite agitated, and he showed me this map he'd discovered in some of his father's old papers, I believe. He was convinced it would lead him to the legendary Alfred's Hoard. I assume you know what that is?" Shadow nodded and she continued, "Kenelm wanted me to confirm what he believed. Naturally, I explained that I and my colleagues at the university would need to examine this map before we could put our names to it. I handed it to two of my PhD students. That was late on Friday afternoon. I've been away at a conference for the last few days. I only returned from London a couple of hours ago, so I haven't spoken to them yet. Is something wrong?"

"Unfortunately, Dr Underhill was found dead at his home earlier today."

"Oh, how awful. The poor man." She paused. "And as the two of you are here, I assume it wasn't an accident or natural causes?"

"That's what we are hoping to find out. He didn't leave his notebook with you too, did he?"

"No, only the map and the other piece of parchment it was attached to."

"What was your opinion of Dr Underhill?"

She hesitated before replying. "Perhaps I shouldn't say so as the poor man is dead, but I found him rather unpleasant. Don't get me wrong he was knowledgeable, far more knowledgeable than some of my fellow academics when it came to the Kingdom of Northumbria and Anglo-Saxon culture. His PhD was on King Aldfrith, and he had an almost encyclopaedic mind when it gave to the various kings and other significant characters from that era, but he was almost too involved. Of course that's not so unusual in the world of academia—plenty of my colleagues have tunnel vision to say the least—but it was as if he couldn't step back. When he spoke about the kings from that time, it was as if they were old friends. He was almost in tears when he spoke about Ivar the Boneless and his raid on York."

"Do you know why he didn't pursue an academic career?"

"I doubt he would have found a position very easily. How can I put it, he held fairly stringent views on various subjects including the role of women and people from other cultures that really aren't acceptable in this day and age." Then she paused and gave a shrug. "Or perhaps he simply realised he could pursue his obsession without the inconvenience of having to teach. I'm sure those overpriced dog biscuits his business sells must have made him a fortune."

"Does Pendle like them?" asked Jimmy.

Dr Shepherd grinned. "Pendle likes anything when it comes to food, Sergeant. I've told Genevieve he'd be just as happy with the cheap supermarket stuff, but she likes to pamper him."

As quietly impressed as Shadow was by his sergeant's ability to recall such details as the name of previous witness's pets, he really didn't want Dr Shepherd to be distracted discussing her partner's dog.

"Did you think this map could be genuine?" he asked. "What did your instincts tell you?"

"Chief Inspector, I generally adhere to the idea that if something sounds too good to be true, it is. However, miraculous events do sometimes occur in the world of archaeology. Naturally, in light of what has happened, I shall do my best to speed things along and should be able to let you know our results in the next day or two."

"Thank you very much. I'd appreciate it. Also, and I'm sorry to have to ask this, but there have been a couple of cases of vandalism in both Museum Gardens and St Cuthbert's at Ellerdale. Someone has been digging holes and we think there's a chance these two incidents could be connected to Dr Underhill's death and his map. Do you think it's possible that someone at the university could have heard about this map and, assuming it was genuine, tried to find the treasure for themselves?"

Dr Shepherd shook her head. "No, I can almost guarantee that, Chief Inspector. Although I'm sure there are plenty at the university who would like to be the ones to find Aldfrith's Hoard—also known as Alfred's Hoard—they would know to go through the proper channels or risk having their findings dismissed. Randomly digging up churchyards and public gardens sounds like the work of an amateur to me."

"Thank you, Dr Shepherd. You have been very helpful. We won't keep you any longer," said Shadow, rising to his feet.

"Not at all, Chief Inspector. Let me show you both out. I expect the main doors have been locked for the night."

"Isn't there a Saxon Museum here in York?" asked Jimmy as they followed Dr Shepherd through the corridors and into the main hall.

"Unfortunately not, Sergeant Chang. We have a small exhibit here to show what happened after the Romans departed our shores. Sadly, the city fell into decline rather quickly and was taken over by an Angle tribe in the fifth century. I could never really understand Kenelm's fascination with the Anglo-Saxon era. Misplaced national pride I expect. Personally, I found them distinctly lacking compared to their Latin predecessors. It was as though we took several steps backwards. Roman villas and bathhouses were abandoned, and we returned to wooden huts and open sewers." She beckoned Shadow and Jimmy over to a stand showing a map.

"Is this York?" asked Jimmy peering at the drawing. "It looks nothing like it."

"It was known as Eoforwic by the Saxons. There are a few places you may recognise." She produced a pen from her pocket and began pointing. "The first wooden minster was built on the site of the old Roman fort for the baptism of King Edwin of Northumbria in 627. After Edwin's death, his successor Oswald began rebuilding the minster in stone."

Jimmy continued to study the map, looking unconvinced as she continued.

"You see there is Aldwark, a street named by the Anglo-Saxons and still in the same location. You have to imagine, Sergeant, the city would have been very different then. The river was the main thoroughfare rather than the roads. All the buildings would have faced the river and boats would have transported goods and people far more than the roads. At this time, the city became quite the thriving economic centre, second only to London. This also meant it was rather an enticing prize and in 866 the Vikings, under Ivar the Boneless captured York and called it Jorvik, as I'm sure you know. Then in 954, King Eadred, half-brother to the previous King Athelstan took it back."

"Oh, I've heard of him. Lance Debenham gave us a bit of a crash course this afternoon," explained Jimmy.

Dr Shepherd raised an eyebrow. "Ah, yes, Lance another of the very committed members of the Ellerdale Saxon Society. I was a little surprised he wasn't with Kenelm when he came to see me on Friday."

"Did Kenelm come alone?" asked Shadow.

"No, he didn't drive. A vicar brought him here. Chap with a beard. I'm sorry I didn't catch his name."

They thanked Dr Shepherd once again and left the museum.

"Wow, I've found out more about the Saxons in the last

couple of hours than I did all the time I was at school," said Jimmy as they headed down St Leonard's Place and back to the station.

"But not much more about this wretched map or its owner or why someone might have wanted to kill him," chuntered Shadow.

"I know Dr Shepherd said she didn't think the two students she gave the map to would do anything to jeopardise their studies, but should I still get their names and run a background check on them?"

Shadow shook his head. "No. Let's wait and see if the map turns out to be genuine first. We've got more than enough to be focusing on at the moment."

When they returned to the station, Jimmy went to set up an incident room while Shadow returned to his office. He shrugged off his old wax jacket, settled into the chair behind his desk and sighed. It had been a long day. His head was full of information, but he was struggling to decide which pieces were relevant to the investigation. He closed his eyes for a second to think. Then a familiar and unwelcome noise made them snap open again. He went to the window and looked outside. Straddling two of the rowing boats that were tied up by Lendal Bridge for tourists to hire, serenading the passing commuters and tourists, was the pirate busker who had disturbed his lunch. As the wind changed direction his singing and the noise from his accordion grew louder. Then there was a knock at his door and Jimmy appeared.

"Tom's sent the results of the background checks to me, Chief."

"Good. You can tell me all about it, but I can't hear myself think with that idiot down there."

Jimmy went to the window and peered down. "You think he'd fall in, swaying around like that."

"If only," muttered Shadow.

"He's not that bad."

"He's terrible but it's his choice of location I object to. If he wants to sing sea shanties he should go to Scarborough or Bridlington. It's out of place here. It's like that chancer who plays the bagpipes outside the station. He should get on a train up to Edinburgh."

"Why don't we get away from the noise and go to Mum's and I'll tell you about it over dinner. She was only asking about you last night."

Shadow gave a slight knowing smile. "You've been eating there every night while Sophie's been away, haven't you?"

Jimmy grinned in return. "I might have been, Chief."

CHAPTER FOUR

Across 6 (4 letters)
Care who wins in this competition of speed

THEY LEFT THE office and the noise of the busker behind and made their way across St Helen's Square and down Stonegate where they found themselves stuck behind a slow-moving party of German tourists.

"I'll text Mum and let her know we're on our way," said Jimmy. "I actually think she was a bit disappointed that I didn't move back home while Sophie was away, but I told her I couldn't leave Fawkes and I couldn't bring him with me because Angela is allergic. It's a shame because he would have liked the company. He's been a bit down recently. I think he's missing Sophie too and it doesn't help that I'm out most of the day, although he does pop downstairs to see Mrs Cowling, our neighbour. She's a widow and gets a bit lonely sometimes, so he calls in most afternoons."

"Very charitable of him," murmured Shadow.

"Oh, that reminds me—I need to text her back and thank her," he said as he started tapping away at his phone again. "She sent me a message earlier to say she'd taken delivery of his food for me."

"The cat has his food delivered?"

"Yep. We get it direct from Underhills every two weeks. It works out cheaper than buying it from the supermarket and Sophie has scheduled deliveries for the whole year, so we never run out, even when we're both really busy with work."

Shadow nodded silently as he tried to understand how Fawkes the cat seemed to be better catered for than he had ever been. They had to pause when they reached the minster as a procession of cyclists whizzed by.

"What's going on?" asked Shadow.

"It's the first day of the Brigantes Race," explained Jimmy. "It's a qualifying race for the Tour de Yorkshire in the summer. Today's route goes round the city and ends at the Knavesmire."

"You would think people had better things to do," grumbled Shadow as the last cycle disappeared and a race marshal stepped aside to let him pass.

Finally, they turned on to Goodramgate and Jimmy pushed open the door of the Golden Dragon, his family's restaurant. The two of them were immediately greeted by a delighted Rose.

"How lovely to see you, Chief Inspector. I hope you are both hungry," she said as she disappeared into the kitchen.

"Starving," replied Jimmy. "I missed lunch when I got called out to Museum Gardens and the chief had his spoilt by a busker."

"Which busker?" asked Angela, Jimmy's sister.

"Some idiot dressed up like Long John Silver," replied Shadow.

"Oh, he was playing outside school today too. I had to move him on. He was disturbing the children," she said, making Shadow wish she'd been with him at the Duke. Then she turned her attention to her brother. "What was happening at Museum Gardens? I saw they'd cordoned off some of the ruins?"

"Metal detectorists have been digging up without permission," explained her brother, his mouth already full of prawn crackers. Rose reappeared carrying a large blue laundry bag.

"Here you are. All washed and ironed," she said proudly. "And there's some groceries to take home with you in the fridge too. I know you will have been too busy to go shopping."

"Thanks, Mum," replied Jimmy as Angela rolled her eyes at Shadow.

"I'm off before she brings out the fatted calf," she whispered. Then calling over her shoulder as she went out the door: "I'm going to meet Tom. See you later."

While Rose continued to fuss over her son, Shadow took his usual place at the table by the kitchen opposite Jimmy's grandfather. The old man gave him a brief nod then promptly produced his backgammon board. The two of them enjoyed a wordless game that Shadow lost as usual. His thoughts returned to the case as Rose arrived with their food and Jimmy joined them.

"What did the background checks show up?" he asked before taking his first mouthful of beef in black bean sauce. Jimmy placed his electronic notebook on the table and began scrolling with one hand and shovelling noodles into his mouth with the other.

"Firstly, Kenelm Underhill received a caution for possession over thirty years ago and another caution a few years ago. This time it sounds like he'd been harassing a local property developer. Simon LeProvost. Mr LeProvost was interested in buying the old village school and what used to be the playing field next to it. Mr Underhill took exception to and I quote 'a damn Norman getting his filthy hands on sacred Saxon land'. That was one of the tamer letters he sent after Mr LeProvost bought some local woodland."

"Interesting. Who else?"

"Well, Edmund Underhill has a string of driving offences, speeding mainly, and he's come close to losing his licence a few times, but the only one with a criminal record is Tristram Prescott."

"The vicar?" asked Shadow in surprise. "What for?"

"Assault. It seems, at his previous parish, down near Glastonbury, he was involved with a local environmental group. They were trying to stop an ancient oak tree being cut down by developers who wanted to build a housing estate. It got a bit out of hand. You know the sort of thing. The environmentalists started damaging the developers' vehicles and chaining themselves to the tree. When one of the building team tried breaking the chains with a bolt cutter, the rev punched him. Broke his cheekbone."

"He didn't look like he had a decent punch in him," muttered Shadow, still surprised.

"Appearances can be misleading, Chief. Tom dug a bit deeper, and it turns out he used to box for his college when he was at uni. He has a motorbike as well. There's a photo of him doing a charity ride in the parish newsletter. He must be one of those trendy vicars."

"That's all we need. Why can't they stick to doing weddings, christenings and funerals? What happened with the assault charge?"

"He was given community service. He pleaded guilty and had plenty of people acting as character witnesses including the bishop, but I thought it was interesting."

"Yes, it is," agreed Shadow, "particularly as we now know he accompanied Kenelm when he went to see Dr Shepherd. Anything else? What about Lance Debenham?"

"Nothing on him but I checked the website at the school he works at in Oxfordshire. He's head of the history department and a housemaster, whatever that is, and he's a bit of an action man too. There's a trip once a year with the Year 8s to the Lake District. It looks like Lance is in charge. There's pictures of him abseiling and kayaking with the kids. He's taken part in endurance challenges for charity too."

"What about Trevor, the security guard?"

"Tom said he was in the army for a few years when he first left school. He left with a dishonourable discharge and has been with Underhills over twenty years."

"What was the reason for the discharge?"

"Tom's checking."

Shadow sighed and shook his head. "There's not much to go on. Let's hope Donaldson or forensics come up with something."

AN HOUR LATER, Shadow and Jimmy left the Golden Dragon. Jimmy, laden down with clean laundry and groceries, headed back to his cat and his flat while Shadow went in the opposite direction to where *Florence*, his houseboat, was moored on the River Ouse. The city was unusually quiet, and he only passed a couple of people as he walked over Skeldergate Bridge. As he took the steps down to the river, he spotted a red canoe floating along. It looked like the ones tourists could hire from down by Lendal Bridge, where the irritating pirate busker had been performing. As the canoe drifted closer, Shadow knelt down and tried reaching for the rope that was tied to the end. For a second, his fingers touched it before it slipped out of his grasp. He stood up and watched the canoe drift away, making a mental note to mention it to the boat hire company. He brushed the damp grass from his trousers as a goose waddled by shaking its head as if despairing at his incompetence.

Once on board *Florence*, he decided to go straight to bed, but despite his full stomach and the long exhausting day, he found he couldn't sleep. After an hour of pummelling his pillow and counting sheep that only succeeded in reminding him of Ellerdale, he got up and poured himself a glass of wine and went over to the low bookcase. He found an old copy of *Le Morte d'Arthur* from his school days and began flicking through. As a boy, he'd enjoyed the tales of King Arthur, Merlin, Guinevere and Lancelot. He could remember running around his mother's kitchen with a wooden sword, pretending to be one of the knights of the Round Table. He'd been disappointed to discover that they weren't real and had eventually lost interest. Yet, it seemed Lance and Kenelm's boyish fascination with the Saxon kings who had ruled parts of ancient Britain had continued into their adult life. Lance had spoken with such passion about them, and Edmund had used the word *obsessed*. Could Kenelm's obsession really have led to his death?

Despite another glass of wine and rereading the whole of Malory's book, he didn't fall asleep until almost two o'clock and was awake again by half past six. He arrived an hour later at the incident room to find Jimmy was already there sipping a takeaway coffee and staring at the computer screen in front of him.

"You're in early," commented Shadow as he shrugged off

his coat.

"I don't sleep very well when Soph's away, so I thought I may as well come in and get started. Trevor has sent last week's CCTV recordings over. I've been spooling through for the last half hour."

"Have you seen anything interesting?"

"Not yet."

"Has Donaldson left a message?"

"No. He told Ben and Ollie that he wouldn't be carrying out the post-mortem until later this morning."

"Typical, he's probably playing golf instead," grumbled Shadow who was starting to miss Sophie too. "And what about Ben and Ollie? Anything from them yet?"

"They confirmed that the dagger or letter opener that was used to stab Kenelm only had his fingerprints on the handle, but that's all. They said they collected loads of samples. Ink, ash, fingerprints, bits of food and especially hair, although they think most of that might belong to Badger. Apparently, Kenelm took that little rowing boat down to Whitby every Wednesday and that was the only time Glenda was allowed to clean the study."

"Allowed?"

"Dr Shepherd did say he had old-fashioned views. Maybe that's what she meant."

"Either way it doesn't sound like we can expect news from Ben and Ollie any time soon."

"To be fair, they went to Camelot Cottage after they'd

finished at Mill House, so they didn't get back until late last night."

At that moment, his phone rang. Shadow went over to the whiteboard while Jimmy took the call. Various photos of Kenelm and his study were now displayed on the board. There were close-ups of the smashed teacup and plates, the glass tumblers from the kitchen and some of the artefacts in the display cabinets.

"That was Natalie," said Jimmy when he'd finished the call. "She said some of the items that were stolen from Camelot Cottage and Mill House have been found. Someone from the village was out walking their dog this morning and found Lance's old computer and the bottles of booze in the beck. Sergeant Thornton and a couple of constables are searching farther downstream."

"Thank the Lord for dog walkers," muttered Shadow. "Let Ben and Ollie know and ask them to get back to the village and take a look." He checked his watch. Bettys would be open now. "I'm going to get some breakfast and give them chance to get there. Tell them we'll meet them later."

Miraculously, Shadow managed to almost finish his full English and two cups of tea before Jimmy appeared at his table.

"You look very pleased with yourself," said Shadow, abandoning his *Yorkshire Post* crossword.

"I am, Chief. Two things have turned up that give Edmund Underhill a motive for wanting his brother out of the way. The CCTV recordings didn't show any intruders, but they did catch Olivia and Edmund Underhill in what I think you could definitely say was a compromising situation."

Shadow raised an eyebrow. "Not very discreet of them. They must have known cameras were there."

"No, I checked with Trevor, and he said they had only been moved there quite recently. Some swallows had started nesting above the previous location and well, they were making a mess on the lens."

Shadow pushed his last piece of egg away and put down his knife and fork. "All right, I get the picture. You said there were two things."

"Yep. When I spoke to Trevor, I asked if he knew if Edmund was going to be at the mill today. I thought you would want to speak to him when we go back to Ellerdale. He said he wasn't yet, but he'd definitely be in later because he'd arranged a board meeting following his brother's death. That made me think it might be a good idea to look at the last set of board meeting minutes—you know to get an idea of what was happening with the company. Trevor said Glenda always took the minutes for any meetings and he'd go and ask her to email them over to me."

"Hold on," interrupted Shadow. "Glenda was Kenelm's housekeeper and his secretary?"

"Yep, and it turns out she's got a cat too, Morgana, who loves the same salmon biscuits as Fawkes by the way." Then seeing Shadow's face: "Anyway the minutes arrived. It was held about six weeks ago and sounded like it was pretty eventful. Edmund raised the issue of selling the business to Percy's Pampered Pets. They are the country's largest producer of pet foods. Edmund and Olivia were keen, but Kenelm wouldn't discuss it. Instead, Kenelm wanted to stop using the mill to produce animal feed and turn it into some kind of Saxon visitor centre. Edmund and Olivia can't have liked the idea because they both rejected it. I phoned Glenda to ask her about it, and she said the minutes were definitely a sanitised account of what happened. The proposal wasn't just rejected but there was a real bust-up. Edmund said the idea was insane, and that Kenelm had lost the plot and should resign and let him be the chairman. 'Stick to burying your head in your bloody books and maps' was the phrase he used. Glenda was quite upset by the whole thing. She had to have a camomile tea afterwards."

Shadow nodded but he wasn't terribly interested in the state of Glenda's nerves. "Where was she when you spoke to her?" he asked.

"At Mill House. Trevor said she'd come in early to tidy and clean the place up. She was too upset yesterday."

"Did she say who would be chairman of the company now Kenelm is out of the way?"

"I didn't ask, but it's got to be Edmund, hasn't it? He's the one sending the staff home and arranging meetings."

Shadow nodded. "If that's the case, not only has Edmund taken his brother's place in the bedroom, but he's also done the same in the boardroom," he said.

"Looks that way, Chief," replied Jimmy, who was still looking very pleased with himself.

"Good, I should leave you on your own more often. Let's get back to Ellerdale and see what Edmund has to say for himself."

However, when they arrived in Ellerdale, Trevor informed them that Edmund hadn't yet arrived at the mill and Olivia was out riding again. So instead they made their way down to the beck behind the mill where they found Natalie with Ben and Ollie. Shadow and Jimmy ducked under the tape that had been strung around the trees by the edge of the beck. Scattered on the ground was a collection of bottles whose labels had become crinkled in the water and a battered and dirty laptop.

"Morning, Chief. Morning, Jimmy," chorused the two scientists.

Shadow gave them a brief nod. "Are these the items taken from Camelot Cottage?" he asked.

"We think so and possibly the bottle from Mill House too. We had a sniff and it's definitely some sort of fruity gin in the bottles."

"Very scientific," grunted Shadow. He wasn't at all surprised the almost-full bottles of Alice's homemade booze had been dumped.

"I've asked Mr Debenham to come down and take a look so we can be sure," added Natalie. "Also, Sergeant Thornton and two constables have gone downstream to see if the bronze items that were taken could have been carried farther along."

"Good," replied Shadow, then turning to the two scientists: "Have you found anything that might help us identify who took them?"

"Sorry, Chief," replied Ben. "They've been in the water so long there won't be any fingerprints and even though the ground here is damper than elsewhere, there aren't any prints from shoes or anything. We think they were probably thrown in the stream from the path. The underside of the laptop is all smashed, it looks like it hit a rock with some force."

Shadow nodded recalling the splash Reverend Prescott thought he had heard. Next to him, Natalie gave a small cough.

"Excuse me, Chief Inspector, but there's something else. I don't know if it's important but Dan Thwaite, that's the man who was walking his dog and saw all this stuff in the beck, mentioned something about Alfred's Cave too," she said.

"What's Alfred's Cave?" asked Shadow.

"It's a stone monument on the hill above the woods. It was built about a hundred years ago in memory of the Saxon king who died."

"The one who is meant to have buried his treasure before the Vikings killed him?" asked Jimmy.

Natalie nodded. "That's right. It was Dr Underhill's grandad who had it built or maybe his great-grandfather. Anyway, it's used as a shelter by walkers and sometimes local kids go up there with a few tins or for a sneaky smoke."

"And why did this dog walker mention it?" asked Shadow.

"Well, at the moment, it's cordoned off as it's unsafe. A couple of stones fell off and we're waiting for some specialist heritage builders to come and take a look at it. But Dan said his dog, Gunner, was going mad up there. Sniffing around and whining. He actually managed to have quick look inside to see if a rabbit or something had died in there, but he couldn't see anything. I thought it worth mentioning in case it had anything to do with what happened at Camelot Cottage and Mill House," she explained.

Shadow nodded and turned to Ben and Ollie. "When you're done here, will you go up there and take a look?"

Then turned as he heard footsteps. Lance Debenham was jogging through the woodland towards them.

"Good morning, gentlemen, Natalie," he called out, raising his hand in greeting.

"Good morning, Mr Debenham. These are the items we found," said Natalie.

Lance's face fell as he looked at the laptop and bottles. "Oh, that's rather a nuisance. I've already put a claim in with my insurance. I was hoping to buy a new one."

"You'll probably still be able to. There's no chance this

one will work again," replied Ollie.

"We will need to hold on to them until the case is closed though," added Shadow.

"Yes, I understand," replied Lance, who had now begun jogging on the spot.

"But you can confirm these are the items that were taken from your house, Mr Debenham?" asked Jimmy, who was taking notes.

"Yes, yes definitely mine," he replied impatiently. "Now if you don't mind, I'll continue with my run or I shall be late for the meeting."

He set off on his run again, then called over his shoulder, "Who was the grandfather of Athelstan?"

"Alfred the Great," Jimmy shouted out.

"Very good, Sergeant. Pleased you were paying attention," replied Lance before he disappeared into the trees.

Shadow watched him go and wondered what meeting he didn't want to be late for, then turned back to the two scientists.

"Jimmy mentioned that you thought there was an awkward atmosphere yesterday when you were talking to the three women in Kenelm's study."

"Yes, it was a bit weird," replied Ben. "After the body had been removed and we'd finished our work, we asked Sergeant Thornton to bring in Mrs Underhill to see if she could identify what if anything had been taken. She wasn't much help to be honest. She said she hardly spent any time in the study, and we'd be better asking the housekeeper."

"Glenda," supplied Jimmy.

"That's right. Anyway, she came through with that other woman with the long grey hair."

"Alice? Why was she still there?" asked Shadow. Ben shrugged.

"We assumed moral support for Glenda."

"She was way more upset than the widow," added Ollie.

"Is that what felt strange?" asked Shadow.

Ben shook his head. "No, it was like they weren't really focusing on what was missing or even that a man they were all close to had been killed. They were just sniping at each other. Glenda told us she thought a ninth-century bronze brooch was missing, then Alice would correct her and say it was actually from the eighth century."

"We asked them about the letter opener. Olivia started telling us it had been a gift from his parents for his twenty-first birthday. Then Alice said it was an item he and Lance had found and tossed a coin for. It went on and on," said Ollie. "In the end, Olivia told Alice, 'I think it would be better if you left Glenda and me to answer any other questions. With Kenelm gone, I really can't see any need for you to be here now or in the future, Alice'."

"She basically threw her out. It was brutal," added Ben.

"All right, thank you. Let us know if you find out anything else," replied Shadow.

He and Jimmy left the other three behind and returned

to the mill. They found Trevor standing next to a classic Morgan sports car in racing green.

Jimmy let out a long low whistle. "What a machine! Is it yours, Mr Thornton?"

Trevor gave a rueful smile. "I wish. It's Edmund's. He inherited it from his dad."

"Kenelm didn't inherit?" queried Shadow although he wasn't especially interested in cars.

"No, Kenelm didn't drive," explained Trevor. He pointed to the large window above the main door. "Edmund's waiting for you up in the boardroom."

They found Edmund standing next to a huge polished oak table, staring out of the window. He turned when he heard them enter. "What's all this about, Shadow? Have you caught my brother's killer yet?"

"Inquiries are still ongoing, sir," replied Shadow evenly. "However, we would like to ask you about the nature of your relationship with Mrs Olivia Underhill."

Edmund narrowed his eyes. "What the hell are you implying? Olivia is my sister-in-law—nothing more, nothing less."

"We have video footage of the two of you together that would suggest otherwise."

"What sort of footage? Where from?"

"From the security cameras here at the mill. Of course we could ask Mrs Underhill but under the circumstances…"

"All right, all right," Edmund interrupted again. "Leave

her out if it. She's got enough on her plate organising the funeral." He gave a deep sigh and gestured to the two chairs as he sat down himself. As Shadow and Jimmy took their seats, he ran his hand through his hair as he considered his next statement.

"Olivia and I have always been close. On the same wavelength you might say. We are actually far better suited than she and Kenelm ever were. He had always been a difficult man to live with, but over these last few years, he became intolerable. It was natural Olivia turned to me for comfort."

"Intolerable how?"

"This obsession of his with the history of the village. All the Anglo-Saxon nonsense. He put it before everything else: Olivia, Cedric, the business. Our father was the same. Obsessed I tell you. It was only because our grandfather created such a solid business that this place has survived their mismanagement all these years."

He waved his hand towards a portrait of a grey-haired severe-looking gentleman hanging over the fireplace.

"Was Kenelm aware of the relationship between you and his wife?"

Edmund shrugged. "If he was, I doubt he cared."

"I understand there was a disagreement between yourself and your brother at a recent board meeting. He rejected an offer from a rival company, and you objected to his idea of turning the mill into a visitor centre dedicated to Anglo-Saxon culture."

Edmund snorted loudly and shook his head. "How on earth did he think that was going to make us any money? Let alone the cost of setting the place up. And who cares about the Saxons apart from him and his cronies. Weirdos the lot of them. Spending time with them has addled his brain. 'It will be our legacy, Edmund; something to honour our history and bring the village together.' That's what he said to me. I told him the mill already brings the people of the village together and pays their wages. Not that he could ever understand the basics of business. When he took over, we were still only producing feed for pigs and sheep. It was my idea to increase our range from feed for farm animal to domestic pets. People treat their dogs and cats like members of the family and are willing to pay a premium for quality. Our biscuits are packed full of nutrients and vitamins, and we provide a tailor-made delivery service too."

"My cat loves them," chimed in Jimmy, earning himself a scowl from Shadow.

"Thanks to me our profits soared," continued Edmund, "and Kenelm could afford to waste his days looking for treasure that probably never existed. What's more PPP were prepared to offer us enough so we could all retire in luxury, and they guaranteed everyone employed here would keep their jobs."

"Are you now the chairman of the company?" asked Shadow.

"Acting chairman. The other board members will have to

elect me officially at today's meeting, but I'm not expecting any objections."

"Other board members?"

"Yes. As well as Olivia and myself, there's Cedric. He won't be here in person obviously, but he is joining us virtually, and that only leaves Lance."

"Lance Debenham is a shareholder?" asked Shadow, realising the board meeting must be what he was referring to as he jogged away.

"Yes. Although he can't always attend meetings. We send him copies of the minutes."

"That's why the minutes noted his apologies," said Jimmy earning himself another scowl.

"The Debenhams have always been minority shareholders," continued Edmund. "That was my grandfather's idea. Centuries ago, the Debenhams had owned the mill you see but lost it through marriage. It was something of a sore point between the families, so my grandfather, by far my most pragmatic ancestor, gifted their family some shares."

"Does that include Alice as well and Lance?"

"It did, but she sold her shares to Lance years ago, after she broke off her engagement to Kenelm."

"The two of them were engaged. When was this?"

Edmund leant back in his chair and exhaled.

"Over thirty years ago now. They were due to be married as soon as she had graduated, but during the last year of her degree she took a module on Celtic history that involved spending a term at Dublin university and time on a dig too. It was while she was out there that she fell in love with a wild Irishman as she put it. She sent Kenelm a letter calling their engagement off and none of us saw her for almost ten years. Then she came back, as mad as ever. Shame it didn't work out really. I always thought they were quite well suited. Both a bit barking. No doubt she was egging him on about opening this Saxon centre."

Shadow glanced over to Jimmy to check he was noting all this down, before asking, "Where were you on the night your brother was killed?"

Edmund didn't flinch at the directness of his question.

"I was at my flat in Whitby and before you ask, yes Olivia was with me," he replied, looking Shadow straight in the eye.

"What time did you both arrive and leave?"

"I left here at about six, Olivia not long after in her own car. We had dinner in a restaurant by the harbour. Our table was booked for eight thirty. We left there at about eleven. The next morning, we both left in separate cars and arrived back here at about eight."

"We'll need the name of the restaurant."

"It was the Blue Lobster," he replied.

"One more thing, Mr Underhill. Reverend Prescott mentioned that Kenelm hadn't been well recently…"

He was interrupted by another snort from Edmund.

"Kenelm was a total hypochondriac. He was always

complaining about stomach pains or feeling dizzy or something else. We'd all got tired of listening to him. Apart from Glenda of course who was always clucking round him like a mother hen."

Shadow nodded and rose to his feet. "Thank you for your time, Mr Underhill."

Jimmy followed him out of the boardroom, down the stairs and into the courtyard.

"What now, Chief?" he asked.

"Let's speak to the widow and check her story matches his," replied Shadow, who had spotted Olivia over by the stables, grooming a large grey horse.

"May we have a word, Mrs Underhill?" he asked.

"I suppose so," she replied glancing over her shoulder but continuing to brush the horse.

"We've just spoken with Edmund Underhill. He confirmed that the two of you are in a relationship."

"He did?" She paused but didn't turn around.

"After we explained that we had some video footage of the two of you together."

"Ah, well I suppose now you know why I wasn't exactly playing my part of the grieving widow yesterday." She put down the brush and turned to face them. "I'm sorry for Kenelm. He didn't deserve what happened to him, but I can't say I'm not relieved he's gone. I wasn't looking forward to a messy divorce."

"Would it have been messy?"

"Aren't they always?"

"Had you asked Kenelm for a divorce?"

"I told him that Edmund and I planned to go away together. He said, 'Jolly good! You could do with a holiday.'" She gave a sharp laugh and shook her head. "I wish I'd met Edmund first, but he wasn't here when I first visited this place. He was working in Hong Kong, seeing something of the world, making a new life for himself. He only came home when his father died and knew Kenelm wouldn't be able to manage running the mill on his own."

She went and filled a bucket from the outside tap. She seemed lost in her thoughts.

"When did you first visit this place?" prompted Shadow.

"My father was obsessed with Anglo-Saxon history like Kenelm. They'd met at some conference or other and Kenelm invited him up here. I tagged along too. I was only nineteen and Kenelm was charming, but now I think about it he was only interested in me because Daddy had traced our roots back to some King of Mercia or Wessex or somewhere. I was naïve. I knew I'd made a mistake as soon as the honeymoon was over. I never really belonged here. I didn't fit in. Kenelm, Lance, Alice even Glenda. They had all grown up together and were like a little clique with their in-jokes about Celts and Saxons. I wasn't remotely interested, but then Ric came along and, well before I knew it, I'd been here nearly ten years living a half-life, until Ed arrived. At first, it was just nice to have an ally but then things progressed, particularly after Ric left home."

"Can you tell us anything else about the items that were taken from your husband's study?"

"Not much. They opened his wallet and took out his cash. He didn't believe in credit or bank cards. A bottle of Alice's godawful gin was missing too and some of his favourite Saxon artefacts. Little bits of bronze. There were some of his first finds."

"Were they valuable?"

"Not especially. Our insurance policy requires us to list anything worth more than a thousand pounds and I know they weren't included but that's as much as I can tell you. Oh, and Glenda said his notebook was missing too and the map, but I believe that's been accounted for."

"What did he use the notebook for?"

"I've no idea. I'm the last person he would have discussed it with."

"Did you know that Alice and Kenelm were once engaged?"

"Of course. I don't think he ever got over the shock of her breaking it off. He even kept a photo in his study of the day they got engaged."

"The one taken on the moors with Edmund and Glenda there too?" asked Shadow remembering the picture he'd seen the day before.

"That's the one. They were up at Alfred's monument. The Saxons even had to be included in his engagement." She paused again. "Come to think of it, my leaving him for Edmund might have been exactly what he wanted. It would clear the way for him to get back together with Alice. If she'd have him."

"Had the two of them rekindled their relationship?" asked Shadow, thinking Alice hadn't appeared particularly distraught by his death if that was the case.

Olivia smiled at him. "What a quaint way of putting it, Chief Inspector. They certainly spent plenty of time together, still behaving like they were students, but whether they were anything more than friends, I can't tell you. Now if you'll excuse me, I need to feed Ivar."

"Good name for a horse," commented Jimmy.

Olivia smiled again. "Edmund chose it to annoy Kenelm." Then seeing Jimmy's blank expression: "Ivar the Boneless was the Viking who captured York from the Saxons."

With that she and her horse made their way into the stable and the two detectives walked back towards the courtyard. Shadow looked up and noticed Edmund had been watching their conversation with Olivia from the boardroom window. He wasn't the only one watching him. Glenda was hovering by the front door of Mill House. She caught his eye and gave him a tentative wave. She looked nervous but at least she wasn't crying today.

"Can we help you, Mrs Kemp?" he asked as they approached her.

"I was wondering if I could make you both a cup of tea? I feel bad that I didn't offer you a drink yesterday, but I was so upset I couldn't think straight."

"That's very kind, but there's really no need, Mrs Kemp," Shadow assured her.

"Oh, but there is. I always offer guests some refreshments. I really wasn't myself. And those two young men who were looking for fingerprints and things were so patient with me while I tried to see what was missing, and I didn't even get them a glass of water," she replied, her face creased with worry as she twisted her wedding ring round and round her finger.

"I'm sure they didn't mind," said Shadow but she had turned her attention to Jimmy.

"What about you, Sergeant Chang? I've got some lovely Colombian coffee you could try."

"That sounds great. Thank you very much," replied Jimmy.

Glenda's face immediately brightened. "You could meet Morgana too. I've told her all about you."

"How does she know what coffee you like?" hissed Shadow as they entered the house.

"I told you we had a quick chat this morning while you were at Bettys. Come on, Chief. It won't do any harm. She might tell us a bit more now she's calmed down."

Shadow trudged after the two of them. Although he welcomed the chance to question Glenda again, he had a feeling with Jimmy and now a cat involved it was going to be a long-drawn-out affair. As soon as they arrived in the kitchen, Glenda began bustling around making the coffee and placed a large plate of chocolate biscuits on the table.

"Olivia and Edmund are the coffee fans. Kenelm and I only ever drank tea," she explained and pointed to a row of wooden boxes lined up by the kettle with neatly printed labels reading, 'rosehip', 'camomile' and 'mint'. Underneath each word was another word written in italics that Shadow couldn't decipher.

"That's quite a collection," commented Jimmy.

"Yes, Kenelm was a real tea aficionado. Alice used to make blends just for him. Mint was his favourite. Would you prefer tea, Chief Inspector? The rosehip is very nice."

"No, thank you. Coffee is fine for me too," he replied. He would have preferred a cup of strong Yorkshire tea, but he had no intention of trying strange herbal blends. "What does it say under the names of the teas?" he asked.

"The Anglo-Saxon or Old English translation or as close as I could find. For example, the hip for rosehip comes from the Saxon word *hiope* and camomile was one of their nine sacred herbs along with fennel and nettle."

Shadow wished he hadn't asked. As he had feared, as soon as they sat down at the small slightly shabby kitchen table, a large fat ginger cat leapt up on to Jimmy's lap. He and Glenda then began a long feline-based chat. Shadow could only sit and silently sympathise with Badger who was curled up in his basket looking miserable about the cat getting so much attention.

"I hope we aren't keeping you. Aren't you needed at the mill, Mrs Kemp? I understood you are also the secretary there?" he asked finally but Glenda shook her head.

"It's fine, Chief Inspector. I was Kenelm's secretary. Edmund sends emails himself and is happy to make his own phone calls and organise his diary. He does it all on his phone," she explained in a tone that showed she clearly didn't approve. "I dare say they'll call me in again when they have the board meeting and need someone to take the minutes. Unless his phone can do that too."

"Did Kenelm go to his office the day he died?"

"No. He didn't go to the mill very often. He left the running of the business to Edmund."

"What about Mrs Underhill?"

"What about her?" asked Glenda and the way her face flushed red before she turned away made Shadow sure she knew about the affair between Olivia and Edmund.

"Did she spend much time with her husband the day he died?"

"They didn't have any meals together. Olivia prefers to make herself something light like toast or a sandwich and eat in the sitting room while she's watching television."

Glenda explained this in the same tone she had used for Edmund's phone.

"I do remember she went to see him in his study in the

morning before she went riding. I think they may have quarrelled. I heard raised voices, but I couldn't tell you what it was about."

Shadow very much hoped she never played poker.

"I understand you helped to identify the items that were stolen from Kenelm's study."

"Yes, although it was such a mess, and I was so upset it was hard to be sure. I came in early today to tidy the place up." She suddenly looked worried. "I hope that's all right, Chief Inspector. The two nice young men in the plastic suits said they had finished."

"That's fine, Mrs Kemp. Did you notice if anything else was missing?"

"No, nothing else. I suppose we should be grateful they didn't get into the rest of the house. I expect they didn't want to go past Badger."

The dog looked up and wagged his tail at the sound of his name.

"Mrs Underhill told us the three pieces of metalwork that were taken were some of Kenelm's first finds."

"That's right. He and Lance found them in the garden right here, when they were testing out their first metal detector."

"Did he often find artefacts? I noticed there were quite a number in the display cases in the study."

"Oh yes, he found all those over the years and all right here in Ellerdale. He used his father's papers to help identify where they might be. His father was quite the local history scholar too and was forever making notes. Every six months or so, I'd bring Kenelm a trunk down. He would go through it and compare his father's notes with his own."

"You brought them down?"

"Yes. Poor Kenelm suffered terribly from vertigo. He couldn't manage the little wooden steps up to the attic where all his father's papers are. Kenelm would begin a new notebook for each trunk. Cataloguing he called it, and more often than not, he'd find something that would lead him to find a piece of metalwork or earthenware."

"And it was one of these notebooks that was also taken from the study?"

"No. The missing notebook is the one he'd been using to jot down all his thoughts on the map he was going to use to locate Alfred's Hoard."

Shadow nodded. He found it interesting that Glenda seemed to find Kenelm's obsession endearing, in contrast to Edmund and Olivia, who both found it irritating.

"Did Kenelm go out anywhere on the day he died?"

"No. He stayed in the study all day except when he gave Badger a run in the garden."

"Did he receive any visitors?"

"Reverend Prescott called around in the morning. I took them a tray of tea and biscuits in at about half past ten. It think he was here to discuss the competition." She tutted and shook her head. "That's all he talks about these days. He even had the nerve to tell me my front garden could do with a tidy. The cheek of it. I've won awards for my hydrangeas."

"What about Alice Debenham?"

Glenda pursed her lips. "Oh, Alice was here but then she's always coming and going. Anyone would think Mill House was her home. It got on Olivia's nerves and Edmund didn't like it either. I heard him telling her off a few days ago. Not that she'd care. Hide like a rhino that one."

"Did she usually enter the house via the study door from the garden as she did yesterday?"

"Oh yes, Chief Inspector. Kenelm's study door on to the terrace was never locked. Everyone who wanted to see him arrived that way. Alice, Reverend Prescott, Lance." She paused. "We always thought Ellerdale was such a quiet, safe little place you see."

"When was Lance last here?"

"Friday morning. I'm afraid they had a bit of a falling-out."

"A falling-out?"

"Yes. Lance was cross with Kenelm. You see Lance had this idea that the two of should go off and try and find Alfred's Hoard themselves, but Kenelm wanted to go through the proper channels. That's why he asked Reverend Prescott for permission to excavate the churchyard near the sundial and why he and the reverend took the map to York later on the Friday so the lady from the university, a so-called expert, could give him her opinion. It's such a shame to think that was the last time Lance and Kenelm spoke to each other. They had been friends for so long and they parted on bad terms."

Tears were beginning to well up in her eyes again. Jimmy stood up and brought the kitchen roll over to her. She smiled at him gratefully, pulled off a piece and began dabbing her eyes. Shadow didn't doubt her grief, but he was more interested in the dismissive way she'd spoken about Dr Shepherd.

"Mrs Kemp, there was a photograph in the study of you, Kenelm, Alice and Edmund. It was taken about thirty years ago. Would I be able to borrow it, please?"

She looked surprised. "Yes, I suppose so. I don't think Olivia will care if you take it. I have more recent ones of Kenelm if you would prefer, though."

"That one will be fine, thank you."

Both detectives stood up as she disappeared through the door.

"Why do you want that photo, Chief?" whispered Jimmy as he gently deposited the still-purring Morgana on to the chair he'd just vacated.

"I'm not sure really," admitted Shadow. "But it caught my eye yesterday."

A second later, Glenda returned and handed over the photograph.

"I understand this was taken on the day Kenelm and Alice became engaged but then that engagement was broken off," said Shadow.

Glenda's expression hardened. "She broke his heart," she replied in a voice cold with anger.

CHAPTER FIVE

Across 7 (3 letters)
Reverse Pam to help you find your way

"ANY THOUGHTS, CHIEF?" asked Jimmy as they left Mill House's kitchen and headed outside.

"Plenty, but none that make much sense. If Kenelm's study door into the garden was always unlocked then why would anyone need to smash it to get in?"

"Well, if it was someone who didn't know the house, they wouldn't know it wasn't locked."

"Surely you would at least try the handle. If we are assuming it was someone from outside the village, a professional thief, who realised Camelot Cottage was empty or perhaps had visited the village previously and found out it would be. They are disappointed with what there is to steal there so they decided to try another larger house in the village," he continued remembering looking across the marketplace from the library window while Lance talked. "Maybe they even noticed Trevor was in the pub. But if they came up here, they would have seen Kenelm in his study. The lights were on, and the curtains were open. Why didn't they target the part of the house that was in darkness? One of the empty rooms?"

"What if they came here first?"

"No. If Kenelm was killed as part of a burglary that went wrong, then I think the thief or thieves would want to get as far away as quickly as possible."

"Maybe that's why they dropped all the stuff they'd taken in the stream. They didn't want to risk anyone connecting them to Kenelm."

"Then why bother taking anything from Mill House at all? Cash might not be easy to trace but some Saxon bits of metal would be pretty risky."

They walked across the courtyard to where their car was parked.

"What if it wasn't someone from outside the village who killed him, but someone he knew and they tried to make it look like a break-in," said Jimmy. "But why? Could it be for that map? Only that wasn't here."

"Unless they didn't know that," replied Shadow who was beginning to wish he hadn't voiced his thoughts. It was difficult enough to try and work out what had happened without Jimmy chiming in every two minutes.

"If it was someone Kenelm knew, my money's on Edmund. With his brother out of the way, he gets Olivia and control of the company. Love and money, two of the oldest motives for murder."

"Hmm," replied Shadow, unconvinced. "Speaking of

money, get in touch with Kenelm's solicitor. Let's find out who would benefit from his death and remember to check with his GP about any health issue he may have had."

Jimmy took out his phone, but as he did so it began to bleep.

"It's a message from Ben and Ollie, Chief. They're up at Alfred's Cave and asked if we want to meet them up there."

"Have they found something?"

"They don't say. I'll text them back and ask."

"Just tell them we're on our way. Knowing the pair of them it will probably be quicker and simpler," grumbled Shadow, rummaging in his pocket for an indigestion tablet. His stomach was already grumbling and now he had to trek up to some stone monument on the moors. To make matters worse it was beginning to drizzle.

They retraced their steps down to the beck, then following Ben's directions, crossed the rickety wooden footbridge between Mill House and the church, then took the winding, partly hidden path that led up through the woods until they emerged on to the moor above the village.

Jimmy shielded his eyes and pointed to what looked like a pile of stones in the distance. "That must be it, Chief."

"It's a miracle Ben and Ollie found it. Neither of them have any sense of direction," puffed Shadow as he had to contend with catching his breath as well as controlling his indigestion.

"To be fair, I think Natalie brought them up here," replied Jimmy, who was striding ahead.

A few moments later, they were at the cave. Natalie was nowhere to be seen but Ben and Ollie were stood outside both with binoculars glued to their eyes. They both turned round at the sound of Shadow's heavy breathing.

"Hi, Chief, Jimmy. It's a great view from up here," said Ben. "You can see the sea."

"We think that might be Whitby Abbey over there to the left," added Ollie.

"This isn't a geography field trip. What have you found?" asked Shadow hoping he hadn't been dragged up here on a wild goose chase. The two scientists hurriedly put their binoculars away.

"Quite a lot but we're not sure how much of it is relevant," Ollie began to explain. He beckoned Shadow and Jimmy to the entrance of the cave. Up close the stone monument was larger than it had first appeared. There was a stone embedded into the ground that explained that it was dedicated to the memory of the Saxon King who died while escaping the Viking raiders. There was also a profusion of yellow and black tape draped around it as well as several hazard signs declaring it to be unsafe.

The structure itself was about seven feet tall, six feet across. The opening was positioned away from the direction of the prevailing wind and from anyone approaching from the village. It was about four feet high.

"We should probably all be wearing hard hats," said Ben

as he ducked low to get through the entrance.

"I'll take my chances," replied Shadow, as he and Jimmy also lowered their heads as they followed the scientists. However, once inside, even Jimmy could stand up straight. It took Shadow's eyes a moment to adjust to the darkness. The only light came from the entrance, which was now mainly blocked by Ollie. Ben and Jimmy both switched on the torches on their phones as Ollie began to explain.

"The first thing we noticed was those dark marks on the ground." He directed his colleagues to shine their lights down on the dusty bare earth floor where there were several black streaks.

"Burn marks?" asked Shadow although he couldn't imagine anyone trying to light a fire in the place—they would be smoked out.

"No, but a good guess. It's actually animal fat."

"That's what Gunner, the dog, must have smelt," added Ben.

"We think someone had one of those disposable barbecues up here and some of the fat from the sausages or burgers or whatever must have spilt out."

"Wouldn't the fumes from those things be dangerous in a confined space like this?" asked Shadow as he wondered if any of this information was going to be relevant to solving a murder.

"It wouldn't be ideal, Chief, but if they positioned in the entranceway, it might be okay," explained Ben. "But the fat isn't all we found. There's a sharp bit of stone over there." He swung his beam of light across the cave. "We spotted a small piece of blue fabric attached to it. We've bagged it up but it looks like it might be nylon. It could have come from a sleeping bag or something."

"So somebody spent the night here?" asked Shadow.

"Natalie said the local kids hang out up here sometimes," said Jimmy.

"Yes. She brought us here and said they usually come up on a Saturday, but they knew not to since it had been declared unsafe."

"Teenagers who want to come up here for a crafty smoke are hardly going to let that bother them," said Shadow. He could feel his patience ebbing away.

"Funny you should say that, Chief. We found some tab ends too. We picked up four and we don't need to take them back to the lab to tell you whoever was up here has been smoking dope."

"Like I said, kids," replied Shadow. "And there's nothing to say the bit of fabric, tab ends and animal fat haven't been here for days."

"Unless my idea about a junkie being behind the break-ins is right," said Jimmy. "Cannabis is a gateway drug after all."

Shadow didn't bother to reply as he placed another tablet in his mouth, but Ollie and Ben had started nodding their heads.

"If you are right, then smoking dope isn't the only connection to Kenelm's death," said Ben. "When we were collecting the piece of blue fabric, we noticed the earth next to it had been disturbed. When we dug down a bit, look what we found." From his pocket, he produced with a flourish an evidence bag, and in the bag was a A5-size leather-bound notebook and several brown objects. "Kenelm's missing notebook and bits of metalwork."

Shadow took a deep breath and tried very hard not lose his temper.

"Don't you think this might have been the piece of information I needed to hear first?" he asked through gritted teeth. He was sure the stress of working with the two scientists would send him to an early grave.

Ben looked crestfallen. "Sorry, Chief. We wanted to set the scene for you. You know, as you weren't here when we found it."

"They were in a ziplock plastic bag and put inside this biscuit tin too," said Ben, producing two more evidence bags containing the said wrapping materials. The tin was from Underhills and was decorated with pictures of various cats, dogs, rabbits and gerbils.

"Hey, I've got one just like that," said Jimmy.

"How long have you had it?" asked Shadow.

"A couple of years now. It was to commemorate their 150th anniversary."

Shadow turned his attention back to the two scientists.

"Are you sure those are the items from Kenelm's study?"

"Well, we need to get someone who knew him to make a positive ID but it looks like it from the description we got of a brooch and two belt buckles. Plus, in the notebook, he's written his name and the date in the front—you know like you did when you were at school. We had a quick flick through. It seems to mainly contain his thoughts about the old map. Questions he was asking himself and a few rough drawings. It seems he thought the treasure might be buried in a church, probably near an altar, and he's written a lot about a sundial too."

"Right, as soon as you have finished with it, we'll need to have a look at it. How long will your tests take?"

"We'll try to get back to you by the end of today, Chief."

"Good. Anything else here to report? Are you waiting to tell me you also found a signed confession from the killer and his current whereabouts?"

"No, Chief," replied the two scientists in unison with a nervous laugh.

"But it's great about the notebook, isn't it?" said Jimmy, ever the diplomat. "I mean it looks like we've got a motive for why Kenelm was killed now. They were after his notebook, and it's got to be someone he knew."

"I'm not so sure," replied Shadow. "It could have been taken before or after he was killed. Glenda said people were in and out of his study all the time. As far as we know, the only person who has shown any level of interest in this map is Lance Debenham and not only was he not here on the night Kenelm was killed but his house was broken into too. Did you find anything of interest at Camelot Cottage?" he asked.

Ben and Ollie exchanged an awkward look.

"We haven't really had time to analyse anything from there or from Mill House yet, Chief," began Ollie.

"We didn't get back to York until late last night. We were going to make a start this morning but then we got called out here again," continued Ben.

"We thought we'd found some shoe prints leading round to the back garden, but they turned out to be Sergeant Thornton's," finished Ollie.

Shadow nodded. It was frustrating but he couldn't really blame them for the delay when he'd been the one to call them out.

"Concentrate on that notebook and let us have it as soon as possible," he replied before turning and beginning the trek back to the village. Jimmy followed close behind as he tapped away on his phone.

"Tom has been in touch. Kenelm's GP hasn't seen him in over five years, so she can't help us, but he's got the details of Kenelm's solicitor. She's based in Whitby."

"Good. Ask if we can see her this afternoon."

"Um okay, but Donaldson has sent a message too. He's completed the post-mortem."

"His game of golf must have been rained off," muttered

Shadow.

"He said he'll be able to see us at two thirty."

"That's gracious of him." He glanced at his watch. It was a little after twelve. "We'll get some lunch in the village then head back to York. Arrange to see the solicitor tomorrow." Shadow tutted. "All this going backwards and forwards. I'm starting to feel like a yo-yo."

He continued on his way as Jimmy began making calls. He reached the path by the beck and looked over his shoulder. Jimmy was still loitering behind in the woods.

"There's no point looking for badgers, Sergeant. They're nocturnal!" Shadow called out impatiently.

Jimmy jogged towards him looking disappointed.

"They probably won't like all this disturbance either," he agreed checking his phone again. Shadow didn't bother to argue that was hardly the point if they were asleep. He crossed over the footbridge and heard someone calling his name. He looked up and saw Reverend Prescott waving at him from the churchyard again.

"What now?" he sighed.

"Chief Inspector! There's been a development."

"What sort of development?" asked Shadow as he walked through the church gate with Jimmy close behind.

"Regarding the disturbance of the sundial," replied the vicar as once again he beckoned them over to the ancient stone. "You'll recall that yesterday I showed you four pieces of turf that had been cut."

Shadow nodded his head wearily. "Well, they appeared to be raised and despite my best efforts they would not lie flat, they looked uneven and as you know I'm keen the sundial looks its best. So, Alice, who was on watch at the time—you remember I told you I was organising a rota so the vandals couldn't strike again."

Shadow nodded again as he wondered if this conversation was heading anywhere.

"Well, Alice and I decided we should remove some of the soil beneath so they would lie flat again then give the area a good watering. In a day or two it would look as if nothing had happened and God willing the judges wouldn't turn up before then."

"It looks pretty good already," said Jimmy who had knelt down to examine the area.

"Thank you, Sergeant," replied Reverend Prescott. "However, the reason the grass looks flat once more is because we removed what was buried beneath and causing the unsightly lumps."

Then with what Shadow considered to be an overly theatrical flourish he produced a cardboard box from behind a gravestone and lifted the lid. Shadow stepped forward to take a look. Inside was a small goblet, two rings and a crucifix. All looked to be made of gold and despite still being covered in mud were clearly extremely old.

"They were buried here?" he asked.

"Yes, Chief Inspector. One item in each hole. We could

scarcely believe it."

"Wow," said Jimmy.

Reverend Prescott grinned at him. "Wow indeed, Sergeant. It looks like poor old Kenelm was right after all. Alfred's Hoard was hidden here all along."

Shadow frowned as he tried to make sense of this latest piece of news.

"Are you certain you didn't see anyone or anything unusual on Monday evening either before or after you noticed the area around the sundial had been damaged?" he asked.

The vicar shook his head slowly. "I finished work on my sermon, and I left the church at about seven thirty. Glenda was here tending her family's graves. I wished her a good evening and went to the Bull to take part in the quiz. I left at closing time and that's when I noticed the damage."

"Why did you come back to the church?"

"Just to check everything was as it should be."

Shadow moved over to the set of nearby headstones the vicar had pointed to. Each had fresh white roses arranged in metal holders.

"These are the graves Glenda was tending on Monday evening?" He read the names. "She was a Thornton as well? Like Sergeant Thornton and Trevor?"

"That's right. Trevor is her cousin, in fact. I believe they were quite close as children. Glenda was often bullied, and Trevor used to stick up for her. For generations, the Thorntons were sextons here, including Glenda's father," he explained.

Shadow nodded as he continued to read the headstones. From the dates, it looked like they belonged to Glenda's parents, grandparents and great-grandparents. He read the details of one out loud. "Agnes Thornton, beloved wife, mother, grandmother, great-grandmother and witch."

"Rather an unusual inscription I grant you, Chief Inspector. But I was told it was meant with love. She provided local herbal remedies to those in need, as well as acting as a local midwife. A remarkable lady by all accounts. You'll notice from the dates she lived to be a hundred. In fact, she was my first burial when I arrived in the village. Quite a nerve-racking experience, I can tell you. The church was packed. Coincidentally, Alice and Lance's father was my second funeral." He turned and pointed to a row of headstones facing towards the rest of the churchyard. "As the Thorntons were sextons, so the Debenhams were the vicars here for several generations. You will notice they are buried facing their flock, so on judgement day, when all the souls rise up, they can lead their flock to heaven."

"Do you know why Lance didn't follow in his father's footsteps?" asked Shadow.

"I believe his father thought he wasn't cut out for it and Lance wanted to pursue an academic career. Luckily for me, I might add." He chuckled. "Kenelm was the church warden and benefice patron. I'm sure he'd have given the job to Lance if he'd wanted it. They were great friends."

"They were but I understand you accompanied Kenelm when he took the map to Dr Shepherd in York—not Lance."

"That's correct, Chief Inspector. After he showed us the map at the meeting of the Saxon Society, I explained that it would need to be verified before the archbishop would grant permission for the churchyard to be dug up. He was keen to set the wheels in motion so to speak, so on Friday afternoon, he hopped on the back of my bike and off we went."

"Forgive me but doesn't sound the safest way to transport an ancient map, Reverend."

"That may well be true, but Kenelm went ahead and made the appointment without a thought to the practicalities of getting to York. Trevor was away, the buses only run in the morning and Kenelm isn't allowed to drive so…"

"Not allowed?" interrupted Shadow. This was a little different to Trevor saying Kenelm didn't drive.

"Something to do with his father's will, I believe. More parental meddling!"

"Is this all really Saxon stuff? What's it made of? Gold or bronze?" asked Jimmy, who was kneeling on the floor photographing the items in the box with his phone. Shadow and the vicar went to join him.

"Alice and I, who if I may say so know more than a little about Saxon history, both believe these items are from the correct period and are almost certainly made of gold," confirmed the vicar who was looking very pleased with himself.

"Has Lance Debenham seen them? We know he was as keen as Kenelm to find the treasure," said Shadow.

"No, he hasn't, Chief Inspector. We only found it this morning. Alice said she would let him know."

"We'll need to take it away and have our experts look at it," said Shadow.

"I understand, Chief Inspector, but we will get it all back, won't we?"

"Once we have confirmed it is the property of the church."

Reverend Prescott looked affronted. "Well, I can't see who else it would belong to. I wanted to inform the press of our discovery. The publicity it generates can only help with the appeal to fix the roof and it would be wonderful if we could show all the items to the judging committee."

"We'll let you know our findings as soon as possible," Shadow reassured him as the vicar produced a prepared receipt from his pocket. Rather reluctantly Reverend Prescott handed the box over to Jimmy. Shadow signed the receipt then they left Reverend Prescott behind and walked round to the front of the church.

"I don't get it, Chief," said Jimmy as soon as they were out of earshot. "Why would someone dig up the treasure and not take it?"

"Maybe they didn't dig the holes to find it but to bury it. The four holes were very exact."

"Are we back to looking for metal detectorists again?

What about the other burglaries? Have we decided there's no connection to this investigation?"

"I wish I knew," muttered Shadow who was feeling more confused by the minute. He had an inkling that everything they had been investigating was connected but he couldn't see how.

"At the moment, I think the most likely explanation is that Kenelm couldn't wait to either hear from Dr Shepherd or get permission from the archbishop, so he came down here and started digging."

"Then he left the treasure behind and someone killed him?"

Shadow shrugged. He knew it didn't make much sense.

"Should we go and speak to Alice?" asked Jimmy. "She was the other person to dig up all this stuff and it seems she was pretty close to Kenelm too."

"I suppose so," agreed Shadow glancing longingly across the marketplace at the Black Bull. They'd probably have stopped serving lunch by the time they finished.

Alice Debenham lived on the edge of the village in what used to be the schoolteacher's house. It was attached to the old school, a stone building that was unmistakably Victorian in design. The old clock was rusty and the windows were all boarded up. The attached house didn't seem to be in much better shape. As the two detectives fought their way through the overgrown garden path to the open front door, Shadow imagined that Tristram would not be including this property on the judge's tour of the village.

"Hello! Miss Debenham! Are you home? It's the police," called out Jimmy.

"Through here," came a voice from inside the house. Shadow and Jimmy made their way into a dingy hallway that felt even narrower thanks to the piles of books and magazines stacked on the floor. The hallway led to a kitchen. To call it chaotic was an understatement. Formica cupboards lined one wall and there was a pine dresser against another. The sink was piled high with dirty dishes. Plants and books covered the windowsills and there was a strong smell of aniseed coming from a pan of leaves and twigs bubbling on the old stove. On the wall opposite the stove were framed black-and-white prints of arty French films. Shadow was reminded of Olivia's comment about Alice and Kenelm still living like students. The back door was open, and the rear garden looked every bit as wild as the front. Today, Alice was wearing what looked like a patchwork smock over leggings. Shadow noticed her feet were bare as she padded across the stone kitchen floor to great them.

"I thought I might be seeing you both again. Did Tristram tell you about our discovery?" she asked.

"He did," replied Shadow gesturing to the box Jimmy was still carrying.

"It looks like Alfred's Hoard was buried under our noses all this time. Kenelm was convinced that was the case. Do you think there's any connection to what happened to him?"

She had the same calm, wide-eyed innocent expression she'd worn when they'd first met her, but Shadow wasn't entirely convinced by it.

"We were hoping you might be able to tell us. Did Kenelm mention any plans he had of digging up the churchyard on Monday evening?" he asked.

"No. I knew that's where he thought the treasure was buried but he never mentioned anything to me."

"But you did visit Kenelm on the day he died."

"Did I, Chief Inspector?"

"According to Glenda Kemp, Mr Underhill's housekeeper."

Alice's face hardened a little. "She's always been a little tell-tale. She hated me dropping by. I'm sure she'd rather have kept Kenelm all to herself."

"You've known each other a long time."

"All our lives. We were both born here in the village within a few weeks of each other. My father was the vicar at St Cuthbert's for many years before Tristram took over. Glenda's father was the gravedigger. And yes, as it happens, I do remember visiting Kenelm. I'd made him a special blend of ginger and chamomile. He'd been complaining of feeling unwell. I thought it might help."

"You don't do anything for indigestion do you?" asked Jimmy.

"Do you suffer, my dear?" she asked.

"Not me," he replied, glancing over to a scowling Shadow.

"Poor you, Chief Inspector. I expect it's the stress of the job. You should consider meditation or perhaps take up yoga. Can I make you a peppermint tea?" she asked looking slightly amused. "Or perhaps you'd like to try a new creation of mine. Dandelion and fennel."

"No, thank you. I'm fine," replied Shadow who had been about to put another tablet in his mouth, but instead shoved it back in his pocket. However, Alice ignored him and went over to the stove to stir the bubbling saucepan. To his horror, she poured the pale-green liquid into three earthenware mugs and set two of them down in front of him and Jimmy.

"I love the humble dandelion and hate it when people simply dismiss it as a weed. A delicious dandelion salad is one of my favourite dishes and fennel is an excellent remedy for all manner of things including gastrointestinal discomfort."

Jimmy took a tentative sip from his mug as Shadow leant farther away from his.

"I understand you are a member of Ellerdale's Saxon Society, Miss Debenham."

"Yes, although I'm more of an honorary member. My interest is primarily with the Celts. Naturally there is something of an overlap between the cultures of the Saxons, Vikings and Celts. However, since I visited Ireland as a student I have felt far more empathy with the Celts. Particularly the women in Celtic culture. I feel they made their presence known in what was a male-dominated society. Now here's an interesting fact for you both. Did you know that King Alfred or Aldfrith as Lance insists we should call him, was the son of an Irish princess called Fin?"

She looked at them both expectantly.

"Um no we didn't, Miss Debenham," replied Jimmy.

"We heard you spent several years in Ireland after breaking off your engagement to Kenelm," said Shadow before the conversation could veer any further off track.

For the first time, Alice looked slightly irritated. "My goodness, the village gossips have been busy. But yes, it's true, we had planned to marry but when I met Cillian, I changed my mind. Kenelm was very understanding, and we remained good friends. I occasionally wondered if I made the right decision but when I returned to Ellerdale, I found he had married Olivia. Kenelm was a loyal and honourable man. He believed in for better or worse and all that."

"Meaning?"

She gave him another of her innocent smiles. "Come now, Chief Inspector. I'm sure I'm not the only one people have been gossiping about. Olivia hasn't even bothered to pretend to grieve and despite being the younger brother, Edmund was always trying to bully Kenelm."

A sleek ginger cat walked across the kitchen worktop as Alice added a spoonful of sugar to her tea and offered some to Jimmy. Shadow wondered when the place had last been disinfected.

"Who's this?" asked Jimmy giving the cat a stroke as she waved her tail at them.

"This is Carti, Sergeant. Short for Cartimandua, Great Queen of the Brigantes, and in my opinion far more impressive than Boudicca, who only ended up getting herself and her followers killed."

Shadow noticed a familiar confused look on Jimmy's face that usually pre-empted a question that would no doubt lead to a longer lecture of Celtic queens, so he quickly stepped in. "Can you tell us a bit more about this map that Kenelm had found?"

"Not really. I only saw it once very briefly. Kenelm announced the discovery at our meeting last week but he was quite protective of it and locked it away in his desk again almost immediately. Lance was desperate for a proper look, but Kenelm said he believed he already knew that the treasure was hidden in the churchyard near the sundial. He thought Tristram was rather mean not to let them go digging around, there and then. Oh, she seems to like you, Sergeant," she said as the cat jumped down and began weaving in and out of Jimmy's legs.

"She looks a bit like my cat, Fawkes. Does she like the Underhill salmon biscuits too?" asked Jimmy.

Alice shook her head and gave him a serene smile. "Oh no, Sergeant. Carti and I are both vegans. Our diets are strictly plant-based."

Shadow tried again. "Did you know that Kenelm and Tristram had taken the map to York to be verified?"

"Not until they returned on Friday evening. I think Kenelm wanted to wait until Lance was out of the way. They had argued, you see. Lance believed it was a waste of time looking at St Cuthbert's. He thought the treasure would have been taken to a larger more important church. It looks like he was wrong and Kenelm was right."

"You were in the study yesterday with our forensics team. Were you surprised by the items that had been taken?"

"I was surprised by the whole episode, Chief Inspector. There was nothing in his reading to show any harm would come to him."

"His reading?" enquired Jimmy.

"I often read Kenelm's palm and his tea leaves. It's another one of my gifts. If you have finished, I'll read yours, Sergeant."

Jimmy handed his mug over, while Shadow silently raised his eyes to the ceiling. He should have been enjoying a steak pie with a pint; instead he was stuck listening to this nonsense, and he doubted if he'd ever get the stench of aniseed out of his nostrils.

"Do you see anything about me moving house? Maybe to somewhere with three bedrooms?" asked Jimmy hopefully.

Alice angled the mug towards her. "I do see a possible relocation perhaps involving water."

"Really? We did see a flat near the river that Sophie

liked." Shadow rolled his eyes as Jimmy lowered his voice. "You don't see death at all, do you?"

A flicker of surprise crossed Alice's face. "Do you fear being killed in the line of duty, Sergeant?"

"No. Not me. My father-in-law is ill. That's what I meant."

She patted him reassuringly on the arm. "Fear not. I see no dark shadows…" then she chuckled as she glanced at Shadow "…except for the one sitting to your left."

Shadow scowled. He had never found his name remotely amusing.

"Would you like me to read your future too, Chief Inspector? Oh, you've barely touched your cup. Come along now, drink up."

Shadow rose to his feet. "Thank you, but I prefer to be surprised, Miss Debenham. I'm afraid we'll have to be going now."

Jimmy trotted out of the cottage after him.

"You hate surprises, Chief," he hissed.

"Yes, almost as much as I hate wasting time listening to claptrap."

As they fought their way back through Alice's overgrown garden, Shadow spotted Carti stalking a sparrow in the hedgerow. It seemed she wasn't the committed vegan her mistress thought. As he finally reached the pavement, he paused for a second and looked back at the cottage.

"How much do you think it's worth?" he asked.

Jimmy looked puzzled. "Are you thinking of moving, Chief?"

"No, but you've done nothing but look at properties for the last couple of months. Don't tell me you haven't googled house prices here in Ellerdale."

"I tried but there isn't anything for sale here. Why?"

"I was wondering how she could afford to live here. Admittedly it's a bit of a dump, but this is a prestigious village; prices must be high. A few classes at the village hall can't make much money. Lance lives in what was the family home. Their father was a vicar in a small country parish, so I can't imagine there was much more to inherit."

"I'll look into it, Chief."

"Good." He glanced at his watch. "We're too late for the pub. Let's see if the fish and chip shop is open."

CHAPTER SIX

Across 4 (6 letters)
Canute and Hilda double up with Unwin and Ric in this place of worship

THANKS TO GETTING stuck behind several packs of cyclists, it was quarter to three when they arrived back in York. As always, Shadow took a deep breath to steady himself before entering the morgue. His years of police work had done nothing to combat his squeamishness and he was beginning to think the fish and chips might not have been such a great idea. Donaldson was waiting for them. Without bothering to issue a greeting, he pulled back the sheet covering the body as soon as they entered the room.

"Well now you are here, I won't waste any time," he began. Shadow, who had been planning to apologise for being late, decided not to bother. "As I said yesterday," the doctor continued, "he was killed by a single stab wound. The blade used was five inches long. It entered the thoracic cavity between the ribs here and the upward thrust meant it went into the heart. He would have bled out in a matter of minutes." He used the end of his fountain pen to point to the entry wound then moved to the marks on Kenelm's neck. "The strangulation occurred before his death and as I suggested the pattern of bruising matches the metal dog's lead that was in the room. Several of his fingernails are broken. It looks like he may have tried to fight back and there are no signs of any sexual activity so I think we can rule out any sort of erotic asphyxiation that the newspapers seem so preoccupied with these days."

"Perhaps you should change your choice of reading material," replied Shadow. "That wasn't a line of inquiry we had considered."

Donaldson scowled. "I've always found you lacking in imagination, Shadow," he sniped.

"Poor guy," said Jimmy shaking his head. "I guess he wasn't strong enough to fight off his killer."

"It may have been a blessing in disguise, Sergeant," replied the doctor with his usual amount of compassion.

"Why? Was he ill?" asked Shadow. Perhaps Kenelm wasn't a hypochondriac after all.

"He was being poisoned," declared Donaldson with a slight smile. He was clearly enjoying the look of surprise on both detectives' faces.

"With what?" asked Shadow.

"*Mentha pulegium*," replied the doctor.

Shadow waited a beat to see if he would elaborate. He didn't.

"Which is?" he asked.

Donaldson gave them both a superior look. "To the common man, it is known as pennyroyal or pudding grass. It's a weed that grows in damp areas. Although it was believed there may be some medicinal benefits from drinking tea brewed from its leaves, it can also be highly toxic. Historically, it was used to induce miscarriages. An old wives' form of abortion, if you will."

"And if a man took it?"

"Symptoms would include dizziness, abdominal cramps, generally feeling unwell. Over time, especially if the dose was increased, it would have killed him. Multi-organ failure."

"Would he have known he was being poisoned?"

"As I'm sure I've told you before, Chief Inspector, I am a doctor not a clairvoyant."

"Was it put in his food?" asked Jimmy, glancing up from his note taking and eliciting another withering look from the doctor.

"I would very much doubt it, Sergeant. As the name obviously suggests, it is part of the mint family. The taste would be rather strong to mask. My guess is that it was put in his tea. According to his housekeeper, when the woman finally stopped weeping, the victim drank mint tea with his evening meal. If you recall, there was a broken teacup in his study. The forensics team are meant to be analysing it, but as usual they have failed to respond to my requests to share their findings. Until they do, I cannot confirm how the poison entered his system. However, that wasn't the only substance to show up in the toxicology report." He paused as he often did when he was about to reveal another piece of vital information. Shadow found it incredibly irritating. "Cannabis was also present in his saliva."

"Wow!" murmured Jimmy as he tapped away.

"Was that in his tea too?" asked Shadow, mentally kicking himself. That was the familiar smell he thought he'd detected in the study before Badger had distracted him, but he didn't recall seeing any ashtrays.

Donaldson gave an exaggerated shrug. He really did enjoy playing for dramatic effect. "The results for cannabinoids are notoriously difficult to interpret. I have sent hair samples for further analysis, but the stains on the inside of his index and middle finger of his right hand would indicate that he has been a longtime smoker."

Shadow nodded as he recalled the thirty-year-old caution while Donaldson continued to pontificate. "However, I found no traces of nicotine. I suggest you speak to your forensic team and ask them if they found anything remotely useful—that's if you can get them to answer their phones."

"Are you able to confirm the time of death without anyone else's assistance?" enquired Shadow. Donaldson always brought the worst out in him. Normally, he would agree that Ben and Ollie were frustrating at the best of times, but there was no malice in their actions, and it irritated him to hear Donaldson criticising them. The doctor scowled again before stomping over to the door and opening it.

"On reflection, I have shortened it to between ten pm and midnight. Now if you will excuse me, I have an important appointment."

"Of course," replied Shadow, more than happy to leave. "Those golf balls won't hit themselves," he called over his shoulder as he stepped out into the corridor.

He was leaving the morgue with more questions than answers. Unfortunately, so was Jimmy.

"Wow! Poison in the tea. It's got to be Alice, hasn't it? Do you remember when we first met her, she told us she was giving a class making herbal teas at the village hall? And Glenda said she was always coming and going. She could be hiding any scratches on her hand with those henna swirls. She could have faked the break-in at her brother's to confuse us. But why would she want to kill Kenelm?"

Shadow held up his hand against the barrage. "And why would she draw our attention to her knowledge of making herbal infusions? She even offered to make me a mint tea. If she'd been poisoning him, she must have been aware that we'd find out after the post-mortem. Also, I would imagine whoever killed Kenelm was wearing gloves since Ben and Ollie have found no sign of fingerprints on the dagger except for Kenelm's."

"Maybe that's what she wanted us to think. You know, like a double bluff. Maybe the poison wasn't working quickly enough so she stabbed him."

Shadow shook his head. "I can't see it. Slowly poisoning

someone is very different to stabbing them. However, if that's the case then it does mean that two people wanted Kenelm dead. Right now, I don't know which theory is more unlikely."

"Glenda prepared all his meals."

"Yes, but of all the people involved, she seemed to care about him the most."

Before Jimmy could add his opinion again, his phone bleeped. He looked at the screen. "That was Ollie. He's finished with the notebook. No fingerprints except Kenelm's and no traces of blood or hair or anything helpful by the sound of things. Looks like you were right about them wearing gloves, Chief. He's left it in the incident room for us."

"Good. Let's see if anything in it will help. And find out who attended these classes Alice held."

They arrived at the incident room to find Tom, a constable who usually worked in the records office, tapping away at the computer.

"What are you doing down here?" asked Shadow.

"Jimmy handed the investigation into the burglaries over to me, Chief."

"Sorry, I messaged him about it last night and forgot to mention it," said Jimmy.

Shadow nodded, Tom was also the boyfriend of Angela, Jimmy's sister.

"I thought I'd base myself down here in case it turns out

the burglaries are linked to the murder."

"Sounds sensible," agreed Shadow, although he thought a connection was becoming less and less likely. "Where's the notebook?"

Tom handed him an A5-size leather-bound book. Shadow opened it carefully. On the first page, as Ben and Ollie had told him, Kenelm had neatly written his name, address and the date. He found it quite touching. As he turned the rest of the pages, he found them filled with drawings and more of Kenelm's spidery writing. He had noted down all his thoughts regarding the map he believed would lead him to the ancient treasure he had been looking for his entire life. His excitement was obvious. Exclamation marks peppered his comments. Several drawings made it clear that he thought St Cuthbert's was the place to start digging. He'd even drawn a diagram that showed the sundial and directions to dig on each side of it.

"Hey, that's exactly what happened," exclaimed Jimmy, who had developed the annoying habit of reading over his shoulder. "It must have been him who dug up the treasure, maybe to check it was there because he couldn't wait to hear back from Dr Shepherd. It would have to have been between about eight and ten o'clock. He could easily have gone down there without anyone seeing him."

Shadow didn't comment but continued to read and tried to make sense of it. Towards the back of the book, Kenelm had written alternative theories for the location of the treasure. He'd crossed them out and added comments such as 'Lance's idea—not possible!' 'Not realistic!' 'What a fool!' It wasn't clear who these last comments referred to, but it was clear that he had considered the abbey ruins in the Museum Gardens as well as Whitby Abbey and Ripon Cathedral as possible locations. He closed the book and put it down, then turned to Tom.

"Can you handle the vandalism in Museum Gardens, too? Visit anyone who lives near there and ask if they saw or heard anything unusual on Monday evening and find out if anything similar has happened at Whitby Abbey or Ripon Cathedral?"

"Okay, Chief," replied Tom, making notes.

Shadow turned to Jimmy. "Let's take all the items that were dug up from near the sundial to Ben and Ollie, then when they have finished with them, arrange for Dr Shepherd to take a look. Let's make sure they are what we think they are."

"I'll call her now," replied Jimmy dialling a number on his phone with one hand and picking up the box Reverend Prescott had given him with the other.

However, when they arrived at the forensic department lab, only Ollie was working there. He looked up in surprise when he saw them.

"Hi, Ollie. These were found in the churchyard in El-lerdale, this morning. Can you take a look and see if there's anything to connect them to our murder victim? We think there's a chance Kenelm might have dug them up first," explained Jimmy, placing the box down on the table in front of the scientist.

Ollie peered inside. "They aren't in the best condition, are they?" he said.

"Neither would you be if you'd been buried for a thousand years," retorted Shadow.

"Actually, it would largely depend on the soil's pH, water content and of course the burial depth," said Ollie. "High acidic levels are terrible for preserving bones, teeth or shells for that matter, on the other hand, the so-called 'bog bodies' from the Iron Age are so preserved thanks to the waterlogged soil and presences of tannins. For example, the skin was in such good condition that the Danish police were even able to take the fingerprints of Tollund Man. Not that the poor guy was suspected of a crime, unless that's why they hanged him." He chuckled then seeing Jimmy's confused expression: "It was probably a ritual sacrifice, not capital punishment. You see…"

Shadow held up his hand. He didn't like the way this conversation was heading. The thought of decomposing flesh was beginning to make him feel queasy again. "Can we save that particular lecture for another time, Ollie? Jimmy has spoken to Dr Shepherd from the Eboracum Museum. She's keen to see these pieces so…"

"Say no more, Chief. Ben and I thrive under pressure."

Shadow raised an eyebrow. He wasn't entirely convinced

this was the case. "Where is Ben anyway?" he asked.

"He should be here in…" he checked his watch "…about eight minutes. He's cycling back from Ellerdale."

"Wasn't there enough room in the car?"

"Oh definitely, but he's in training for next year's Brigantes Race and as part of the route goes through Ellerdale he thought…"

"That took priority over a murder investigation?" enquired Shadow.

"No, Chief, of course not," replied Ollie quickly. "But like I said he should be here in less than ten minutes. That's assuming the wind speed doesn't increase. He could beat his last time by thirty seconds. You know it's all about getting that life-work balance…" He trailed off when he saw the look on Shadow's face.

"And they do say physical exercise improves mental function," chimed in Jimmy.

Shadow shook his head and turned away. If his sergeant was correct, it would take running several marathons to improve how his forensic team functioned. "Anything else to report?" he asked without expectation.

"Only about the cigarette butts we found. It wasn't tobacco they were smoking but pretty strong weed. What's more I think it was Kenelm who was smoking them."

"That would tie in with what Donaldson told us," interrupted Jimmy.

Shadow scowled. It was bad enough that Ollie had wasted time talking about cycling and soil acidity rather than pass on this new information. He didn't want him getting distracted again.

"Why do you think it was Kenelm not local teenagers?" he asked.

"I'll have to wait for the results to come back from the lab before I can be certain but when we were in his study, I noticed there were some cigarette papers in one of his desk drawers. They weren't the normal cheap ones most people use to roll their own; these were made of organic hemp. The tab ends we found had the same print on them."

"Isn't hemp part of the cannabis family too?" asked Jimmy.

"That's right. They used to use hemp paper to make banknotes too," agreed Ollie.

"Did you find anything else in his study that made you think he was a smoker?" asked Shadow as his patience continued to ebb away.

Ollie's face creased in concentration. "There were some matches on the mantel over the fire, but we didn't find an ashtray or any cigarette ends. Actually, one of the crime scene guys found traces of ash on the carpet but assumed it came from the open fire. I'll make a note to get it analysed." He tapped at his computer before continuing. "That isn't all though. Not all the cigarettes had been smoked by Kenelm. I think a woman had been smoking with him."

"Traces of lipstick?" guessed Jimmy.

"Not quite, but traces of some kind of wax residue was on some of them. I've had a quick look under the microscope and I think it might be propolis." Then seeing the detectives' blank expressions: "It's bee glue. They use it to make lips balms. Again, we'll need to get it analysed properly."

"On that subject do you have the results for tests on the mint tea Kenelm was drinking. We think it might contain pennyroyal."

"Sorry, Chief, not yet. Donaldson asked us about it too. There were loads of it growing down by the stream in Ellerdale though. We took a sample while we were down there."

"Good. We'll leave you to get on. Let us know as soon as you have anything else."

Shadow mulled this new information over as he headed back to the incident room with Jimmy close behind. As they made their way back to the incident room, they met Ben, hot, sweaty and in his cycling clothes.

"Hi, Chief, Jimmy. I shaved twenty-five seconds off my best time."

"Congratulations. The showers are in the basement. I suggest you visit them," replied Shadow without stopping.

"Heading there now, Chief!" he called out as he jogged down the stairs. Shadow watched him go. He was wearing the same sort of Lycra shorts and top that Lance had been dressed in when they first met. He was also wearing cycling gloves.

"Have we checked Lance's alibi? Was he definitely in Durham?" he asked.

Jimmy opened his electronic notebook and scrolled through. "Yes, he had rented an Airbnb for a couple of nights. Someone spoke to the person he was renting from. She confirmed she met him at about four o'clock on Monday afternoon to hand over the keys and that he called her the next morning to let her know that he had to return home and wouldn't be staying for the second night. Then he called again, to say he had left his bike behind and would return later to collect it. Remember he told us he was going up there on Tuesday evening. I also spoke to the taxi driver who picked him up outside Whitby station on Tuesday. Turns out it was Natalie's dad. Small world, eh? What's up? You don't look convinced."

"Do you remember when we saw him for the second time at his cottage? He spoke about Kenelm's death and said something like, if only Badger could have protected him. The child gate had been put up after he left to go on holiday. How would he know that Badger hadn't protected his master?"

"Because Kenelm was dead, Chief. Or maybe it was just a figure of speech. Maybe he'd overheard something in the village. All the workers from the mill were in the pub," replied Jimmy with a shrug.

"Glenda said he and Kenelm had argued."

"But he wasn't in Ellerdale on Monday night. Edmund had disagreed with Kenelm recently too. My money is still on him."

Shadow nodded as he continued to think, and Jimmy carried on talking.

"What do you think about the cigarettes, Chief? It's got to be Alice smoking dope with Kenelm, hasn't it? But what I don't get is, they are both adults and it's unlikely, even if they were caught, that they would be prosecuted for personal use in a private residence. Why did they go sneaking up to the monument for a smoke?"

"I don't think they did, but I do think someone wants us to think they did. I know you've already done a background check on everyone but get in touch with the police in Ireland and see if they have anything on Alice from when she was living there."

"Will do, Chief. Hey, I've just had a thought. Alice is a vegan. Are vegans allowed honey?"

"It's not really my area of expertise."

"By the way, this Tollund guy Ollie mentioned. He isn't a Saxon as well, is he?" asked Jimmy.

"No, he lived in the fourth or fifth century BC or BCE as you would say."

"And he was murdered?"

"Probably but for now can we please focus on the current murder we're investigating."

THAT EVENING, SHADOW had arranged to have dinner with Maggie. As was often the case, she was running late. Her hair was still wrapped in a towel when he called for her at the flat above the laundry she owned.

"I won't be a minute. I was chatting on the phone to Sam and lost track of time," she called as she disappeared back up the stairs. "I'm expecting a delivery from the supermarket. He's running late too. Let him in when he arrives, will you?"

Less than a minute later, there was a cheery rat-a-tat-tat on the door. The delivery driver's bright smile faded when Shadow opened the door.

"Maggie not around?"

"She's busy. Come through," replied Shadow, taking one of the crates of shopping from him. The driver followed him through into Maggie's kitchen.

"Sam coming home, is he?" he asked, referring to Maggie's son, who lived in Spain.

"How do you know that?"

The delivery man nodded his head at the crate he'd just deposited on the worktop. "Peroni beer, tubes of Pringles, two sirloin steaks, not to mention all the extra milk and fruit juice. Oh yes, I always know when Sam's home."

"I see," commented Shadow as he began loading the cartons of milk into the fridge.

"Oh yes," continued the delivery man when he returned with the second crate, "that's the thing about this job, you certainly get to know your regular customers and all their routines."

He seemed to be expecting some sort of response.

"It must be interesting," Shadow offered as a reply.

The delivery man who seemed in no great hurry nodded. "Oh it is, but quite a responsibility too. I've got one customer who gets through two bottles of scotch, a bottle of vodka and twenty-four cans of Special Brew every week. I feel like I should say something, but it's against company policy. Then the other day, one of my customers went and died. I knew something was wrong. Every morning, she filled the bird feeder up with peanuts but when I got there it was completely empty and the curtains where closed. I rang the doorbell and there was no answer. I went round the back and that's when I saw her through the kitchen window. She'd collapsed in the hallway. Turns out she'd been dead for three days, poor thing. Her heart apparently. She seemed fit enough, but she did tell me she took an aspirin a day so perhaps I should have known. Anyway, I'll get your last crate."

With that he disappeared again, leaving Shadow thinking.

"Do you only deliver to York?" he asked when the delivery man returned with the final items.

"That's right. I cover anywhere within the ring road, but some of our lads go as far as Easingwold and Selby. Since the

Scarborough branch closed, we go right out to the coast as well."

He left with a wave. As Shadow closed the door, Maggie shouted down. "Put anything chilled in the fridge and frozen in the freezer, then leave the rest to me?" Shadow did as instructed, then phoned his sergeant.

"What's up, Chief?"

"Check to see if our burglary victims received regular grocery deliveries."

"Groceries? You mean like from the supermarket?"

"Yes. The delivery drivers must cover a fairly big area. Find out if that could be the link we're looking for."

"Oh I see what you mean. Like the idea about ordering the currency but from a different angle. They might have included suntan lotion or something and got talking and told the delivery driver they were going away and how long for."

"Yes, yes, that's the idea. Anyway, I'll leave it with you. Get Tom to look into it if you've got too much on your plate."

"Okay, Chief. By the way, Edmund identified the bronze items Ben and Ollie found. They are definitely the ones that used to be on Kenelm's desk."

"Edmund identified them, not Olivia or Glenda?"

"That's right. I phoned the house, but he answered. He said all calls were being put through to his office and asked me to email the photos to him. Maybe he knew more about his brother's life than he first admitted. See you tomorrow, Chief. Have a nice evening?"

As he finished his call, Maggie appeared and quickly put away the rest of the shopping.

"Did Martin say if anything was missing? I didn't have chance to look at the email receipt."

"Who?"

"Martin. The delivery driver."

"No. I think it's all here. He's a bit overfamiliar, isn't he?"

"He's friendly—I like that. After all they know all our dirty little secrets. Like if I buy Aunt Bessie's Yorkshire puddings rather than make my own."

"Why would you need to do that? You're a good cook."

"Thank you, kind sir." She gave a mock curtsy before putting the Pringles and beer into a cupboard. "Let's go. All this talk of food has made me ravenous."

That evening they were dining at Catania's, one of Shadow's favourite Italian restaurants and only a little farther down Goodramgate. Maggie had ordered a risotto and he'd chosen the steak boscaiola. As usual the food and the bottle of Valpolicella was delicious, but his mind was still on the case.

"You're very quiet tonight," Maggie commented as they'd almost finished their main courses.

"I was just thinking."

"You know, sometimes you can voice your thoughts. It's

called making conversation. Admittedly, you may consider it a strange idea, but others have tried, and it seems to have caught on."

Shadow gave a wry smile. He was used to her teasing him. "I was thinking about the case. Our victim was once engaged to a young woman who left him for an Irishman, then returned to the village after he'd married another. I was wondering how he felt about that."

"It sounds like the plot of one of my romance novels. Is your victim the owner of the pet food mill out near Whitby?"

"Yes. How do you know?"

"His picture was all over the front of this evening's paper."

"MacNab didn't waste any time," grumbled Shadow, wondering who had tipped off the local hack.

"Well, it's very sad that he's dead but I thought he looked a bit of a wet blanket. I don't blame her for running off with a hunky Irishman. The accent alone would make me go weak at the knees."

Shadow smiled. "We've no evidence to say he was hunky or otherwise."

Gino, the owner of the restaurant, came to clear their plates. Shadow ordered an espresso and Maggie a green tea.

"You'll never sleep if you drink that," she chided. "Tea is much better for you."

"I'm a bit off tea at the moment," he replied without

adding that they suspected that was how Kenelm had been poisoned.

However, it turned out that as usual, Maggie was right. Whether it was the strong coffee or the thoughts of the case whirling in his head, at one o'clock the next morning, he was still wide awake, listening to Frank Sinatra and sipping another glass of red wine. Jimmy had sent him a message to say that the Blue Lobster in Whitby had confirmed that Edmund and Olivia had dined there on Monday evening and that Dr Shepherd had been in touch and would like to see him first thing in the morning. Hopefully, she would have news about the map.

He flicked through some of the case notes he had brought home with him. Tom had printed off some information about the abbey that had once stood in Museum Gardens, as well as St Cuthbert's in Ellerdale, Whitby Abbey and Ripon Cathedral. All had been founded by the Saxons and played their part in helping the pagan country become Christian. It was all probably very interesting for someone like Kenelm, who was obsessed with that era, but he was struggling to see where it fitted into the case.

His stomach had begun complaining again, so he downed the last of his wine and padded over to where he'd left his old wax jacket draped on the back of a chair. He reached into his pocket for an indigestion tablet, but instead found the photo he'd taken from Kenelm's study. He'd forgotten all about it. Now he stood it on the table and reached for a notebook. He stared at the much younger faces of Edmund, Alice and Glenda. Seeing Edmund looking so happy and carefree, it was hard to imagine him killing his brother but perhaps Jimmy was right, and he was the most obvious suspect.

He wrote down the three names on the notepad in front of him, then added Olivia, Tristram and Trevor. Six names in total, but of those he couldn't think of anyone who had both motive and opportunity. Olivia and Edmund may have wanted Kenelm out of the way but they both seemed to have an alibi, although they needed to check the times more thoroughly. Alice and Glenda could certainly both have poisoned him, but why would they want to and could either of them have stabbed him? As for Tristram, he didn't have much of an alibi but again why would he want Kenelm dead? The same could be said for Trevor. Then there was Lance may have wanted to find the treasure, but he was up in Durham and as much as Shadow disliked the man, he couldn't be in two places at once. Shadow sighed. Perhaps it was a good thing Tom was still looking into the burglaries. It could be an outsider after all.

The next morning, he bypassed Bettys and instead headed to the Roman Museum on St Leonard's Place. The receptionist directed him to a small room at the back of the museum where Dorothy Shepherd was waiting for him. It was brightly lit but there were no windows. On the Formica-topped table in front of her lay the box containing the items dug up from St Cuthbert's and two mouldy and ragged pieces of parchment that were partly sewn together.

"The map is a fake, Chief Inspector," she said without any preamble. "An excellent fake but a fake nonetheless. Take a look for yourself."

Shadow peered closely at the parchment. On one piece was a very basic drawing showing squares and crosses and a dotted line. To Shadow it looked a bit like a floor plan. The other piece was covered in writing that he couldn't even begin to decipher.

"This piece is genuine," Dr Shepherd began to explain as she pointed to the piece covered in writing. "It refers to King Aldfrith and his encounter with the Vikings. My guess is it was written by a monk, possibly from Whitby Abbey, shortly after the king's death. However, this piece is faked. The symbols and drawings look correct for the time but when we analysed the ink, it was modern. It's the parchment that made it so difficult for us. It's definitely from the Anglo-Saxon period as is the thread they used to join the two pieces. It's the sort of thing that you would usually expect to discover if you were excavating a monastery. I'd love to know where they got their hands on it."

"I think I might I know," murmured Shadow as an idea started to come together in his mind. "Does the written part say where Aldfrith's treasure was buried?"

Dr Shepherd shook her head. "It's much vaguer than that. It talks about the king fleeing and mentions the gold he had with him. Then there's a bit that says after he was slain those who were true to him buried him and all that was worthy of him in a most sacred place. Unfortunately, it doesn't say where that place was."

"And Kenelm would have been able to read it?"

"Oh yes, I'm sure of that. As I told you before, he really was quite the expert."

"But there isn't a specific mention of St Cuthbert's at Ellerdale or the sundial there?"

Dr Shepherd shook her head. "No. It could refer to any sacred or religious place in the area, but I think Kenelm was so fixated on the village church because of the diagram that we now know is fake." She used her pen to point to the map. "It looks like the interior of a church with this oblong being the nave and the treasure being shown as being buried near the altar, if we assume this rectangle with the semicircle is the altar, but it could also be the famous sundial and the oblong, the churchyard." Shadow nodded as she continued to talk. "Which brings me to the items you discovered yesterday," she said moving over to the box.

"You've had a chance to look at them already?" he asked, a little surprised.

"Yes indeed. I was most excited when I heard from Sergeant Chang. As soon as your forensic chaps had finished with them, I dashed over, and I can tell you that these are the real McCoy!" He half expected her dance a jig, she sounded so excited.

"This is definitely Aldfrith's Hoard?" he asked.

"It's definitely gold and it's definitely Anglo-Saxon. I can't give you an exact date until we carry out more tests and we would need to study contemporary sources to find a definite link to Aldfrith, but all in all very thrilling. Such a shame Kenelm isn't here to see it."

Shadow nodded. "We were told he was often finding Anglo-Saxon artefacts, even in his own garden. Does that sound unusual to you?"

"A little," she replied, "but then Ellerdale was quite a prominent settlement in the area at that time and Kenelm was certainly very dedicated to discovering all he could about that part of history."

"If you have finished with the map, can I take it for forensics to have a look at?" he asked. "By the way, who knows it isn't genuine?"

"Myself and my two colleagues. The PhD students I told you about. That's all."

"May I ask you all not to tell anyone else about it?"

"Certainly." She paused. "You think the map is the reason Kenelm was killed."

"I think it could be and I would rather the killer continues to believe it is real."

"Very well," she replied, using her gloved hands to place it into an artefact box. "But if you don't find the owner of the genuine piece, my department at the university would be very happy to give it a home."

"Of course. I'll keep you informed," he promised.

CHAPTER SEVEN

Down 3 (8 letters)
Initially, Alfred is sure the rat is valuable

AFTER THANKING DR Shepherd for her help, he left the university deep in thought and headed to the station. However, as he walked through the main entrance, he met Jimmy coming down the stairs. He was smiling broadly.

"Morning, Chief! Lots to report back, most importantly Sophie's dad is doing really well. He's got some feeling back in his left arm and she's coming home on Saturday."

"That is good news. Pass on my best wishes. Where are you going?"

"Actually, I was coming to find you. I thought you might have gone to Bettys after seeing Dr Shepherd. We've got an appointment to see Kenelm's solicitor at ten o'clock so we should probably get going."

"All right," replied Shadow, although slightly miffed that he would be missing out on the breakfast he had been looking forward to. "You can update me on the way." He handed the artefact box to the constable behind the reception desk. "Get that sent to forensics, will you."

"What's that?" asked Jimmy, as they headed out the door.

"Kenelm's map. Turns out it's a fake or at least half of it is."

He told Jimmy everything Dr Shepherd had said as they made their way to the car park.

"Okay, Chief, how is this for a theory," began Jimmy when Shadow had finished. "Kenelm finds the piece of parchment with the writing in his dad's things and a blank piece. He has a hunch that Aldfrith's Hoard is buried in the churchyard but needs something to get permission to dig, so he fakes the map. But the rev tells him he needs to get it verified. Kenelm knows Dr Shepherd will say it is a fake, so he waits until it's dark and he's on his own, goes digging near the sundial and finds the treasure. Someone sees him, follows him home, kills him then panics and makes it look like a break-in and, because they know Lance is away, they decide to target his house too, so we think it's a break-in gone wrong."

"Then how did the treasure end up buried again?"

Jimmy frowned. "Maybe when they panicked, they put it back there. If they don't have it, it's harder to link them to the crime. They could always dig it up again later."

Shadow shook his head as he climbed in the car. "I'm not saying I don't agree that Kenelm could have faked the map, but I'm not convinced by the rest of it. Who would be hanging around the churchyard at night and just happen to see Kenelm?"

"Reverend Prescott. This is part of what I wanted to tell you. Tom made a few inquiries about what happened at Museum Gardens and two people who have flats down Marygate both reported hearing a motorbike at about the same time that warden arrived. I was thinking, he and Kenelm might have discussed other locations for the treasure, and he decided to have a look on his own. He brought Kenelm to York on the back of his bike, remember?"

"Yes," agreed Shadow, "but a lot of other people have motorbikes in York especially those takeaway delivery drivers that seem to be everywhere these days."

"To be fair, I think they mainly use mopeds and scooters, Chief."

"Either way, they are a damn nuisance, and most people wouldn't know the difference if they heard them."

"True," conceded Jimmy, "but there is more. Ben and Ollie got in touch. The results came back for the mint tea residue that was still in Kenelm's broken cup. It definitely contained toxic levels of pennyroyal oil. And do you remember those two tumblers on the draining board in the kitchen at Mill House? You got me to bag them up."

Shadow nodded.

"They said they had found traces of brandy and decent sets of fingerprints on both," continued Jimmy, "so we ran them through the database and one set is a match for Tristram. His are on file after his arrest for assault."

"What about the other glass?"

"We haven't got a match yet but they aren't Kenelm's."

Shadow frowned as he processed this information. Tristram must have been at Mill House, drinking with someone either just before he went to the pub at about eight o'clock or after he left. Glenda, Edmund and Olivia were all meant to have left by about seven o'clock. But who was he drinking with if not Kenelm?

"He didn't show up on the CCTV footage at all?"

Jimmy shook his head. "He must have entered the garden by the bottom gate near the beck and taken the path up to the kitchen door."

"Have we found out anything more about Trevor Thornton?"

"His dishonourable discharge was in 1999."

Shadow raised an eyebrow. "A year before the ban on homosexuals in the army was lifted."

"Exactly and neither he nor Tristram have ever married."

"We might be getting ahead of ourselves but it is interesting and it would explain how Tristram spotted the digging by the sundial. I thought it was odd when he said he just happened to be there. He could have cut through the churchyard on his way back from Mill House. But if they are in a relationship, would they really need to keep it secret in this day and age?" He paused and thought for a second. "Trevor fitted the child gate. He must have left his prints near where it was screwed to the door frame and it's unlikely that anyone else would have touched that area. I remember Ollie was kneeling down taking some prints from the door frame. Get him to see if they match the ones on the glass."

"I'll message him when we get to Whitby. Good thinking, Chief!"

"Thank you, Sergeant."

Jimmy ignored his sarcasm and ploughed on. "There's something else about Tristram and Trevor too. They both attended Alice's class on Nature's Bounty at the village hall last week. That was her first class, and it was on natural remedies. The bit on the website mentioned how you can get aspirin from willow bark. It sounded pretty interesting."

"I don't suppose there was a reference to pennyroyal as well was there?"

"Afraid not and the only other attendees were Lance's neighbour, the one with the hearing aid, and two sisters from Whitby who are in their eighties."

"I suppose it's possible Tristram and Trevor were only there to show support to Alice," he said as he mulled over this new information. "Anything else?"

"Some of the team looked into Glenda's background. Craig's father was a university lecturer. He was much older than Glenda and married when they first got together."

"Which university?"

"Durham."

"Glenda was at Durham university?" he asked in surprise. She hadn't struck him as being particularly academic and Durham was second only to Oxford and Cambridge.

"Yes, studying history of art and architecture but she didn't graduate. It seems Craig's arrival messed that up. She and this Professor Kemp guy married just before he was born but divorced a couple of years later and she returned to Ellerdale. The professor died a few years after that, when Craig would have been five or six."

"Shame she didn't finish her degree," murmured Shadow.

"I also checked out Alice Debenham like you asked. The school and her cottage is or rather was owned by Kenelm Underhill. She rented it from him, but I was thinking if they were still close, she could be paying less than the market rate. I don't know who inherits it now though, but I'm guessing the arrangement might not continue."

"Hopefully the solicitor will be able to tell us, but if this very convenient arrangement depends on Kenelm being alive then it ruins your theory that she was the one who poisoned him."

Jimmy sighed. "I guess you're right. But before I found out about the rent, I also made a few inquiries in Ireland about her too. You know, to see if she had a job out there and had been paid redundancy or had a pension or anything?"

"And?"

"Apparently, she helped out on some archaeological digs and volunteered at a museum in Limerick. It's only a small place and they focus on the Celtic period. I gave them a ring and got chatting to a really nice lady called, Neve. She's the volunteer co-ordinator and remembered Alice straight away. She said she 'left under a cloud'."

"What does that mean exactly?" asked Shadow, wishing for the hundredth time that his sergeant had a fast forward button.

"Well, it seems her split with the Irish guy was pretty acrimonious. He left her for a younger woman, one of his students. Alice packed her bags, but he accused her of taking some of the artefacts they'd unearthed together during one of the digs. According to Neve, there was a full-blown slanging match out in the street between the two of them. The locals still talk about it. Then after she'd left, the museum found some pieces from their collection were missing. There were about half a dozen items that couldn't be accounted for."

"Did they report it to the police over there?"

"No. They were items that weren't important enough to be part of the main display and had been kept in storage. They couldn't say for sure when they'd been taken and certainly not that Alice was responsible, but Neve said they'd never heard from her again, which she thought was strange when she'd been so involved."

"Did she say what they would have been worth?"

"She thought altogether less than a thousand euros but she didn't know about the items from the dig. So I did a bit of digging myself, Chief…" Shadow suppressed a groan

"…and there's an auction house in Harrogate that have specialist antique sales. Over the last few years, they have had some pieces from the Celtic era. They were all described as 'property of a lady' but I added up the sale prices and it came to over five grand."

"You certainly get a lot done when you can't sleep."

Jimmy grinned. "I'll probably crash out for a week, when Soph gets back. Should I contact the auction house and see if it was Alice?"

"Yes, but right now it's not a priority. All we've learnt makes it less likely that she's our killer so let's focus on finding out who is."

They drove along in silence for a few minutes before Jimmy spoke again.

"Limerick sounds really nice, and I loved Neve's accent. I was thinking, I might try and book a weekend away there, you know after all the stress Sophie has been through with her dad. As long as we've finished with the investigation, of course, Chief."

"Good idea," agreed Shadow with a sigh. He didn't begrudge Sophie a holiday, but it would mean he'd have to deal with Donaldson on his own if there were any unexplained deaths while the pair of them were away. He thought for a moment.

"When you next contact Tom, check to see if Alice could be connected to our other burglaries."

Jimmy gave him a puzzled look. "You really think she

could be involved with them?"

"No, but if she really is a thief, it's worth checking." He paused. "And something about the break-ins at Camelot Cottage and Mill House doesn't feel right," he murmured. In truth, he'd been thinking out loud, which was unlike him. He had an inkling Alice was involved, but he was struggling to see how exactly. "Check to see if she has an alibi for when the churchyards were dug up too."

Jimmy gave a wry smile. "You're really not a fan of hers are you, Chief?"

"I find her and her brother very irritating. Unfortunately, that isn't a criminal offence."

They arrived in Whitby at quarter to ten. Jimmy found a parking space on West Cliff and they made their way down the famous Khyber Pass and crossed the bridge over the River Esk into the old town. Below them an array of boats bobbed up and down, from canoes to trawlers and even a couple of sailing yachts. It was a bright but breezy day and the narrow streets were already busy with tourists heading to the beach, fishermen unloading their catches and groups of goths heading up to the ruined abbey that still dominated the town from its position high on the cliff.

The offices of Loxley and Co Solicitors were on Church Street in a tall thin stone building squashed between a second-hand bookshop and a jewellers selling the famous Whitby jet. Shadow wasn't sure what he'd been expecting when he met Patrica Loxley, Kenelm's solicitor, but it certainly wasn't the sixty-something woman with short white hair streaked with purple, puffing on a vape and wearing a T-shirt with a sequined skull on the front beneath her black trouser suit.

"Call me Patsy," she instructed as she ushered them to the two chairs opposite her desk that was piled high with legal papers. "And you're here to find out about Kenelm Underhill's will. Normally, I would do the reading after the funeral but under the circumstances I'll give you the general details. He left most of his money to the village church, St Cuthbert's."

"Not his son or wife?" interrupted Jimmy who was taking notes.

"No. Olivia gets Mill House. Edmund gets his shares in the business. All his Saxon artefacts—he refers to them as his most treasured possessions—go to Miss Debenham."

"Alice not Lance?" queried Jimmy.

"That's right. I've got a list of them somewhere. They had sentimental value apparently." She began rummaging through the papers before selecting one and passing it over the desk to Jimmy. "You know their history, do you?"

"Yes," replied Shadow. "It sounds like he still carried a torch for her after all these years. We understand Kenelm owns the house she lives in too."

"Yes. Both the school and the schoolhouse are held in trust by the Underhill family, but Kenelm controlled the trust. The Underhills built the school for the mill workers back in the 1860s, I think. The local farmers' children benefitted too of course."

"Do you happen to know how much rent Miss Debenham pays?"

"I do, Chief Inspector. I drew up the lease. She pays one pound a month."

Jimmy gave a long low whistle. "That's crazy!"

"I should add that I made that very point to Kenelm, but he ignored my advice."

"Because he still had feelings for Miss Debenham?"

"I really couldn't say, Chief Inspector. He may have simply felt sorry for her. Her father cut her out of his will when she disappeared off to Ireland. That's why Lance got Camelot Cottage."

"A while ago, a Mr LeProvost wanted to buy the old schoolhouse. Is that correct?"

"Yes. He was property developer from Leeds and bought a place up on the moors. I believe he'd made rather a lot of money converting industrial buildings, mills and warehouses and so forth into flats. He'd bought a large area of woodland he wanted to build on too. Edmund was friendly with him and was very keen to sell the old school to him, but Kenelm wouldn't hear of it. Do you know, I don't think I have ever known the two brothers to see eye to eye."

"Kenelm wrote some letters to Mr LeProvost," said Shadow.

The solicitor grimaced. "Yes. He got rather carried away

there. It wasn't only letters. There was talk of staging a protest. Tying himself to trees and so forth. LeProvost's rather lovely sports car was damaged too, although there was no evidence that was Kenelm."

"Because Mr LeProvost's name sounds a bit French?" asked Jimmy.

She shrugged. "Oh, I believe Kenelm had gone to the time and trouble to trace his family tree and discover his ancestors came over with the Normans. However, you are correct, Sergeant Chang, it still isn't much of an excuse for Kenelm's behaviour. But then his behaviour often didn't make much sense to me. Although in the case of Mr LeProvost, he was egged on by those who should have known better."

"Lance Debenham?" ventured Shadow.

"Yes, Chief Inspector, and Alice and even the local vicar."

"Ah, the Saxon Society," said Shadow.

"The four of them were talking about setting up an encampment in the woods in question until LeProvost got wind of it and had his solicitor send a letter warning them off. I think Kenelm might have still gone along with it, but Lance and the vicar got cold feet. Understandable, I suppose—unlike Kenelm, they both need to work."

"I understand Kenelm and his brother disagreed on another matter more recently. Edmund wanted to sell the mill. Can you tell us anything about that?"

"Not much. It's not really my area of expertise, but our commercial department who are based in Hull are dealing with it."

"So the sale is going ahead? I thought Kenelm vetoed it."

"He did. Although according to Edmund, he couldn't get him to discuss it properly. Kenelm only wanted to talk about turning the mill into some sort of museum or cultural centre. However, I believe Edmund and Olivia had negotiated with the other party and they agreed to buy their shares only. They wouldn't get such a good price, but they would still walk away with a decent amount."

"When was all this agreed?"

She put her glasses on and began to flick through the large desk diary in front of her.

"Let me see now. Ah yes here it is. Edmund came to see me six weeks ago. That's when I advised him to speak to the team in Hull."

"Was he angry about the situation?"

"Angry? No, frustrated perhaps, but then that was his default setting when it came to dealing with Kenelm. I often thought it was a shame he wasn't the older brother. Kenelm wasn't really suited to responsibility."

"What about Mrs Underhill? Did she ever visit you, possibly to discuss a divorce?"

"Ah, so all the rumours I have been hearing are true, are they? Well, in answer to your question, no I don't think I have ever spoken to Olivia privately and certainly not about divorce, but then if that was something she was considering, I image she would prefer to find a specialist family lawyer who was unconnected to Kenelm."

"Had Kenelm ever been in trouble with the law before? I'm thinking in particular about his drug use."

Patsy raised an eyebrow and took a long drag on her vape before releasing a white plume that filled the room with a liquorice smell and reminded Shadow of Alice's fennel tea.

"As you knew about the business with LeProvost, I assume you also know he has no convictions in that regard." She paused, then sighed.

"I don't suppose it matters now, but there was an occasion, before my time, back when my father was the family solicitor. Lance and Kenelm were both home from university one summer and went on a bit of a rampage through the village. Stole a car, wrecked some floral displays, tried to dig up the old sundial and injured a villager. Both high as kites. Kenelm's father managed to get it all swept away, paid for Mr Thornton to have private medical care but the poor chap never walked again."

"Which Mr Thornton would this be?"

Her forehead creased as she tried to recall. "Gosh! Now you're asking. There are so many of them in Ellerdale. I remember this one was a widower who had a son in the army. He was away at the time of the incident, I think."

"Is this the reason Kenelm wasn't allowed to drive?" asked Shadow.

"That's right. Both he and Lance had to promise never to get behind the wheel again or risk being disinherited. Lance's father was livid. There had been plans for Lance to continue his academic studies. He was going to do a master's and then a PhD, but his father refused to fund him, so instead he got his PGCE and became a teacher." She paused and took another drag on the vape. "He was rather an odd fish, the father I mean. Very controlling. My father thought he was worried about the family reputation. His father or grandfather, I can't remember which, had been accused of stealing from the church. You know what small communities can be like, they don't forget things. However, he and Lance must have made up eventually as he left him the cottage but his will had lots of codicils. There was something about if Lance should act in a way to besmirch, he used that very word, the family name, Alice gets the cottage. I could probably dig a copy of it out for you if you want and send it over."

"That would be helpful, thank you," replied Shadow. "Going back to Kenelm's will for a moment. Is there no mention of his son?"

"Cedric? No. No mention. He doesn't get a bean."

Jimmy looked up from his notetaking in surprise. "Because he's a New York banker who doesn't need the cash?" he suggested.

"No, Sergeant, because he is gay," replied the solicitor bluntly. "Kenelm didn't approve of what he called his son's lifestyle choice and from what I can tell Cedric was quite happy not to have his father involved in his life. In fact, I doubt very much if he will even bother returning for the funeral."

After thanking her, Shadow and Jimmy left Patsy's office and gratefully stepped out into the street and the fresh air.

"It's a bit weird leaving all his money to the church and not his wife and son, isn't it, Chief?"

"Dr Shepherd did warn us he had old-fashioned views. As for Olivia, maybe he knew what she was up to with his brother, or maybe he was worried about his soul. I'm more interested in whether Tristram knew the details of the will and if Trevor is the type of man to bear a grudge," replied Shadow but Jimmy didn't reply. He looked around for his sergeant. Jimmy was a few feet behind him. He had his nose pressed against an estate agent's window.

"Property is loads cheaper out here," he said.

"Are you thinking of asking for a transfer?"

"I couldn't do that—you'd miss me too much." Jimmy laughed as his phone began to bleep. He checked the screen. "It's Tom."

"Any luck with the supermarkets?"

"Yes and no, Chief. Two of the victims used the same supermarket and got regular weekly deliveries."

"But not the other two?"

"No."

"Oh well, it was worth a try."

"He's also heard from the warden at Whitby Abbey.

They had an intruder who also dug some holes on Tuesday night."

They both automatically raised their eyes to look at the ruins above them.

"It gives me the creeps. I keep expecting Dracula to come swooping down."

"You are aware that Dracula isn't real, aren't you, Sergeant?"

"I still think it's spooky."

"Well, you had better get yourself up there and see if there could be a connection to whoever was digging in Museum Gardens and at St Cuthbert's."

"Are you not coming, Chief?"

"You must be mad if you think I'm about to climb one hundred and ninety-nine steps for what may well be some petty vandalism. I'll go to the restaurant and check on Edmund and Olivia's alibi."

"The mussels there are meant to be really good," said Jimmy with a grin, as he headed towards the Abbey.

"So I hear," replied Shadow, thinking this could be adequate compensation for missing breakfast.

Disappointingly though, the Blue Lobster was not serving lunch that day. However, he did manage to speak to the charming young Greek couple who ran the place. They both remembered Olivia and Edmund. Apparently, they were regular customers. They confirmed they had dined there on the evening Kenelm was killed, although they had been twenty minutes late for their reservation and they left at eleven when the restaurant was closing.

"Did you happen to overhear them talk about returning to Ellerdale that evening?" he asked.

The young woman shook her head. "Oh no, Chief Inspector." She lowered her voice. "Between them they had drunk a bottle of champagne and a bottle of wine so they would both have been over the limit."

Shadow thanked them and left, although he wasn't sure that being done for drink driving would worry you too much if you were planning on killing your brother or husband.

He left the harbourside restaurant and began making his way back through the cobbled streets. He found a second-hand bookshop at the foot of the steps that led up to the abbey. He went in to browse while he waited for Jimmy to return. Amongst the shelves of dusty paperbacks, a copy of *Le Morte d'Arthur* caught his eye. He picked it up and began turning the pages. He was so deep in thought, he didn't notice when Jimmy appeared next to him.

"I thought I saw you in here, Chief. Did the restaurant confirm Edmund and Olivia were there?"

"They did but they left at eleven. Half-cut by the sound of things but they could still have made it back to Ellerdale. We can't rule them out yet. What did you find out up at the abbey?"

"It's the same as what happened in York and in Ellerdale, Chief. Four holes dug around what was the location of the altar. It must have happened between about six o'clock on Tuesday night and nine the next morning."

"No, CCTV, I take it?"

Jimmy shook his head and noticed the book he was holding. "Are you going to buy that?"

"No. I already have a copy."

"Is it any good? I've only seen the Monty Python film. That was pretty funny."

He immediately starting humming 'Always Look on the Bright Side of Life'.

"That's the wrong film," snapped Shadow. Hunger was making him even more irritable than usual. He sighed as he put the book back on the shelf. "I could be clutching at straws, but in some versions of the legend, Arthur is killed by his son. We are sure Cedric Underhill is definitely in New York, aren't we?"

"Definitely. Tom had a video call with him. He said he didn't seem that upset about his father's death, but after what Patsy told us, I'm not surprised. Apparently, he was in this really cool office overlooking Central Park. He must be raking it in. I bet he's got an amazing apartment too." He paused. "If this story about Arthur is a legend, doesn't that mean it probably isn't true?"

"Yes," agreed Shadow with a sigh. "Let's go and get something to eat. Then we should go to Ellerdale and speak to Glenda and Alice. See if we can get any closer to finding out who was trying to poison Kenelm."

"By the way, Chief, I had an idea about the burglaries on the way up to the abbey, so I gave Tom a ring," began Jimmy as they left the bookshop.

"What idea?"

"Well, do you remember how all the victims had a pet?"

"Yes, three dogs and a cat."

"That's right. The lady with the cat spoilt our theory about the boarding kennels. Well, I remember speaking to her and she apologised for rearranging our meeting, but her daughter takes her shopping once a week to Northallerton. They make a day of it apparently. You know have lunch out and all that."

"And?" interrupted Shadow impatiently.

"I should have remembered before I got Tom to ask her about the supermarket deliveries because she told me she gets all her essentials there except the cat food Mr Tibbs likes. She gets that delivered from Underhills. I told her about Fawkes at the time, but then I forgot about it, but now…"

"Now there could be a link to those burglaries and the two break-ins at Ellerdale after all," interrupted Shadow.

"Yep. Tom is on with phoning them all again now."

They turned a corner, and Shadow groaned as a familiar noise met his ears. "He must be following me," he complained pointing to the accordion-playing pirate next to the ice cream kiosk.

"He's not that bad and he's certainly drawing quite a crowd," replied Jimmy who had begun swaying along.

Shadow grunted. "I'm going to get some fish and chips to eat on way back to the car. Do you want any?"

Jimmy made a face. "I don't think I could stomach them two days in a row. I might get an ice cream though."

"Please yourself," muttered Shadow as he went to join the queue that was already snaking outside the door of the Magpie Café, down the steps and on to the quayside.

When he stepped back outside clutching his warm haddock and chips nestled in their newspaper, he spotted Jimmy with his phone clamped to his ear in one hand and a ninety-nine in the other. He was nodding vigorously as he listened. As soon as he spotted Shadow, he grinned and gave a thumbs-up sign.

"Bingo, Chief!" he declared triumphantly as soon as he hung up. "That was Tom."

"Good news, I take it," replied Shadow as he plunged his wooden fork into a vinegar-drenched chip.

"Yep. All four of our burglary victims had regular deliveries of pet food from Underhills. They provided a description of the delivery guy that matches Craig Kemp. Two of them even knew him by name." He paused. "They seemed to think he was a nice guy. It's sad really. I've got Glenda's home number. Do you want me to call and see if he's at home?"

"No, I don't want to give him any warning. Let's go out to Ellerdale and see what Mr Kemp has to say for himself. Get Sergeant Thornton and Natalie to meet us there," replied Shadow.

"It's got to be Craig who did Lance and Kenelm's place too," said Jimmy when he'd finished on the phone again. "It's too much of a coincidence otherwise. Kenelm's death must have been a burglary gone wrong after all."

Shadow frowned as he continued to eat. Although he agreed that it was quite a coincidence, he was also of the opinion that thieves didn't like to make a mess on their own doorstep. As he was thinking about Craig, he noticed something that looked suspiciously like a CD sticking out of his sergeant's pocket.

"You didn't?"

Jimmy gave an embarrassed shrug. "Lots of other people were buying them and on the sleeve there's a history of all the songs. He doesn't just do sea shanties but folk songs as well. Actually, can I put it in your pocket, Chief? I've got too much stuff in mine—it doesn't really fit."

And with that he removed the CD from his leather jacket and placed it into the large square pocket of Shadow's wax jacket. He was about to protest, when he spotted Edmund Underhill striding towards them.

"Busy with the investigation into my brother's death, gentlemen?" he asked sarcastically as he eyed their ice cream and fish and chips.

"We had an appointment this morning with Miss Loxley," replied Shadow, trying not to choke as he swallowed down a particularly large chip and wishing his sergeant didn't have bits of chocolate flake around his mouth.

"Then you will know all the gory details of Kenelm's will and I expect you have been checking up on me at the Blue Lobster too. When we left there, we returned to my apartment." He pointed to a tall building overlooking the harbour that had once been a bonding warehouse. "I'm sure the town must have some CCTV should you wish to check our movements any further."

"I understand you had a disagreement with Alice Debenham recently?" enquired Shadow, suddenly remembering something Glenda had said that at the time had seemed unimportant.

Edmund looked a little taken aback by this change in direction, but he gave a brisk nod. "As I'm sure you have probably already discovered, Chief Inspector. Alice was renting her cottage from Kenelm. If you can call it renting. I would say she pays a peppercorn rent but that would actually be an improvement. Her cottage is actually owned by the family, but Kenelm made this arrangement without consulting me. All the bills for the cottage—council tax, buildings insurance, utilities—are all paid by the business."

"Isn't that rather an unusual arrangement?"

"That may be the understatement of the year, Sergeant. A few days ago, we received the electricity bill for the last quarter, January to March. It's always been on the high side, but this time it had gone through the roof. It was more than the bill for Mill House. Anyway, I knew it would be pointless discussing it with Kenelm so I confronted her about it."

"What was her response?"

"What it always is. She didn't care as long as she was all right. Don't let all that hippy-drippy stuff fool you, Shadow, underneath it all she's as hard as nails. But now Kenelm has gone, she'll be out on her ear. She and her brother won't take advantage of my family any longer. That's what the Debenhams have always done. They're like the damn cats everyone seems to have in the village. Always out for number one. Give me a dog or a horse any day." He paused and looked Shadow straight in the eye. "You might not think I'm any better for the way I've behaved with Olivia, but let me tell you this: I loved my brother. I found him infuriating, but I also felt quite sorry for him. He was so insular. He barely left North Yorkshire let alone the country and he didn't trust anyone who was different to him. He had his demons too. He may have been the older one, but I've always looked out for him. Believe me or don't believe me, but I didn't kill my brother."

"His demons being the amount of cannabis he smoked?"

Edmund gave a rueful smile. "And I'm sure you don't need to be a chief inspector to work out who was supplying him." With that he turned on his heel and stalked back towards the harbour.

"Well, he was pretty convincing, Chief," said Jimmy taking another bite of his ice cream as Edmund disappeared from view. "He was my number-one suspect. At least until we heard about Craig. You didn't ask Edmund about him."

"No. Let's keep as many people in the dark as possible." They retraced their steps up the Khyber Pass. "Tell me more about the items that Alice might have stolen and possibly sold on. When was the last Celtic antique you told me about sold in Harrogate?"

With one hand, Jimmy scrolled back through his notes. "About eight months ago. A small bronze bull statue dating from the first century. It sold for £475."

"Well, that wouldn't last long. Even if she got everything else for free, she still needs something to live on. When we've finished with Craig, we'll pay Alice a visit."

Realisation suddenly dawned on Jimmy. "Of course. The electric bill. Heat lamps to grow dope."

"Exactly—and brewing that damn fennel concoction when we were there to mask the smell."

"But hold on. I know she shouldn't be supplying but if we are focused on finding Kenelm's killer, doesn't this make her less of a suspect? She relied on him for her home, and it sounds like he was her best customer. Why would she want to poison or stab him?"

Shadow dumped his now empty newspaper wrappings in a bin. His sergeant had a point, but this case had so many loose ends, he was determined to tie up any he could.

"Perhaps she thought he might do something to expose her without meaning to," he suggested almost to himself. "Or perhaps she knew about the artefacts he was leaving her and thought they might be worth killing him for."

Jimmy began reading from the list Patsy had given them.

"Anglo-Saxon bronze strap-end—£75, Romano-British silver trumpet type brooch £250, Anglo-Saxon lead loom weight—£50, Anglo-Saxon bronze ring with spiralling bezel—£65, Anglo-Saxon gilt trefoil dagger pommel cap—£1k." He paused and shook his head. "Imagine collecting all of this. It's weird, don't you think, Chief? I mean, all this stuff about the Saxons. Does it really matter? It all happened over a thousand years ago."

"It mattered to Kenelm Underhill and possibly whoever killed him. That's the point," replied Shadow as they climbed into the car and headed back to Ellerdale.

CHAPTER EIGHT

Across 10 (8 letters)
Lance brings the reed and ivy to me

THEY ARRIVED IN the village to find Sergeant Thornton and two uniformed constables waiting for them by a police car in the middle of the marketplace.

"Have any of you seen Craig Kemp this morning?" asked Shadow.

"No," replied Sergeant Thornton, "but he was in the Bull last night and downed enough to sink a battleship. His bedroom curtains are still closed. I'd be surprised if he's surfaced yet."

They all looked over to the row of cottages behind the pub. The upper window of number two did indeed still have its curtains closed.

"Is there a back door?" asked Shadow.

"Yes, Chief Inspector. If you go down that ginnel along the side of the pub it takes you to a footpath that runs along the back gardens of Underhill Row."

"We plan to arrest him for breaking and entering. We also want to question him about Kenelm Underhill. If he should make a run for it…"

"Don't you worry, Chief Inspector," interrupted Sergeant Thornton puffing out his chest, "I'll go through the pub garden and round to the back of Glenda's cottage. He won't get past me," he declared confidently before trotting off towards the pub. Shadow turned to the two remaining constables.

"When Sergeant Chang and I are inside the house, park the marked car outside and wait for us to bring him out," he instructed, then he and Jimmy crossed the square and approached the Kemps' cottage. It was by far the best-kept and prettiest of the three houses. Pale-pink roses entwined themselves around the black wrought-iron railings and up the wooden trellis on either side of the cream front door. Two window boxes were crammed full of white pansies and either side of the gravel path were two pink hydrangeas in large stone urns. Jimmy knocked on the front door.

"I'm coming," called a female voice and a few seconds later, Glenda's anxious face appeared.

"Oh, hello, Chief Inspector, Sergeant Chang. Can I help you?"

"May we come in?" asked Shadow.

"Yes, yes of course." She moved to one side and the two detectives stepped straight into the cottage's sitting room that was as neat and tidy inside as it was outside. The walls, carpet and two small sofas were in various shades of cream. Hanging on the walls were scenes from the tales of King

Arthur painted in watercolours, except for above the fireplace where there was the biggest television screen Shadow had ever seen. It looked completely out of place and he could only assume it was for the benefit of Glenda's son.

"Go through into the kitchen," said Glenda and, as she closed the door behind them, Shadow could hear the sound of the police car pulling up. The kitchen was also a sea of cream from the dresser to the blind half covering the window. Through this window, Shadow could see the garden with its greenhouse, neatly mown lawn and more urns and terracotta pots holding magnolias, camellias and the hydrangeas that he now recalled Glenda had said she'd won prizes for. Standing like a sentry at the rear gate was the rotund figure of Sergeant Thornton. Glenda didn't appear to have noticed him as she bustled around the kitchen.

"I remember you both prefer coffee to tea, isn't that right? Now, if I've got the hang of this, I can offer you an espresso, cappuccino or a latte," she said as she began fiddling with a large and complicated-looking coffee machine on the worktop.

"We're fine, thank you, Mrs Kemp," replied Shadow. "Would it be possible to speak to your son, Craig?" he asked.

"He's asleep, I think. Is it important?" she asked her face creased in worry again.

"Yes, I'm afraid it is."

She went to the stairs in the corner of the room and called up. "Craig! Are you awake? There's someone here to see you." Nothing. "I'm sure he'll be down in a minute," she said.

"While we are waiting, could you tell us a bit more about the mint tea Kenelm was so fond of? Did you always make it for him?"

"Yes, at least almost always. He drank gallons of it. Alice was always having to keep us topped up."

"Is the tea still in the wooden boxes in the kitchen at Mill House?"

"No, I'm sorry, Chief Inspector. I cleared all his teas away the other morning not long after you left. Olivia asked me to. She said they made the place smell. I suppose they did a bit. Craig! Did you hear me?" she called again, as Shadow silently chided himself for not taking a sample of the tea when he last spoke to her. From above their heads came a soft thud, then Morgana came creeping down the stairs.

"I'll go up and give him a knock. He's a very heavy sleeper," said Glenda and trotted up the steps. Shadow turned to Jimmy. He expected him to be fussing over the cat, but his sergeant was frowning and seemed preoccupied by some of the other shiny hi-tech gadgets in the kitchen.

"I think that could be the coffee machine from the first burglary, Chief," he whispered. "I remember because it's the one I wanted, but Soph said two and a half grand was too much."

"For a coffee machine!" exclaimed Shadow, as Jimmy shushed him. "Thank God you married an intelligent woman. What's wrong with a kettle?"

"Hold on! I've got a note of the serial number. I can check," said Jimmy as he carefully picked up the gadget. "That air fryer and the massive TV look like the ones that were nicked too."

"Surely he wouldn't be stupid enough to hold on to everything he stole?" muttered Shadow, but before Jimmy could reply, Craig came plodding down the stairs. His mother who was looking more anxious than ever followed behind. He was wearing jogging bottoms and a *Star Wars* T-shirt. He yawned, then belched and flopped down on to one of the kitchen chairs. Even from where he was standing, Shadow could smell the stench of stale beer. He thought he may need to revise his last comment.

"What do you want?" asked Craig yawning again.

"We have reason to believe that you may be involved in a recent spate of burglaries," replied Shadow.

"Oh dear," whispered Glenda.

"Nothing to do with me," said Craig leaning back in his chair with a confident air.

"Several of the victims were customers of Underhills. You regularly deliver to their houses."

"So?"

From behind Craig, Jimmy, who had been engrossed on his phone gave him a silent thumbs up.

"So how do you explain that an item that was taken during one of these burglaries, is now sitting in on the worktop in your kitchen?" asked Shadow.

Craig twisted his bulky frame round and glared at Jimmy. "What item?"

"This coffee machine has the same serial as the one that was taken three weeks ago," said Jimmy.

Craig shrugged. "I don't know anything about that. I bought it cheap from a bloke who didn't want it anymore."

"Who was this bloke?" asked Shadow.

"Didn't catch his name. Some bloke down the pub. I thought Mum would like it."

"He's always spoiling me," chimed in Glenda. "He bought me that air fryer too. I'd seen them on of those cooking shows. They're ever so good."

"That's enough, Mum," said Craig quietly. Jimmy moved over to the air fryer and started checking that too.

"Can you tell us where you were between ten o'clock and midnight on Monday?" asked Shadow.

Craig shrugged again. "I can't remember."

"You don't remember where you were the night Kenelm Underhill was killed?"

"Oh, Chief Inspector!" interrupted Glenda again. "You can't think my Craig would do anything to hurt Kenelm. He has always been very good to us. He treated Craig like a son, didn't he, love?"

The young man rolled his eyes. "Oh, give it a rest, Mum. He was our boss. Yours and mine. Nothing more nothing less, and he wasn't very good at that. He didn't even treat

Ric like a son. Edmund has always been more of a dad to him. God knows what he did all day. But I didn't kill him."

"We didn't say you did, Mr Kemp, but we would like to know where you were on Monday night."

"In the Black Bull like everyone else."

"And after the pub closed at eleven?"

"I came home."

Shadow looked at Glenda. "Can you confirm that?"

But before she could open her mouth, Craig jumped in. "Leave her out of it. She was asleep."

To the side of him, Jimmy gave a small cough, then nodded when Shadow gave him an enquiring look. Glenda was watching them. "Oh dear, Chief Inspector, I'm sure it's just a coincidence."

"I'm sorry, Mrs Kemp, but finding two items of stolen property at the same residence is more than just a coincidence. Over to you, Sergeant."

Jimmy began reading Craig his rights, while Glenda looked close to tears.

"Don't worry, Mum. I'll be okay," said her son as he was handcuffed and led out to the waiting police car. Shadow raised his hand and waved to Sergeant Thornton to tell him he could leave his post.

"Is there anyone we can call to come and sit with you, Mrs Kemp?" he asked.

"No, thank you, Chief Inspector. I think I'd rather be on my own. When will you let Craig go?" she asked.

"We'll keep him in custody until he's been able to answer all our questions," he replied without adding that if it turned out he had stabbed Kenelm, he wouldn't be coming home for a very long time. He wrote down the number for the York police station as she slumped down on to the seat her son had recently vacated and a tear slid down her face.

"I'm very sorry," he said with genuine sympathy as he handed her the piece of paper. "We'll have to check for other items that we believe may have been stolen too."

He arrived back outside as the police car taking Craig to York pulled away. Jimmy was finishing speaking to the custody sergeant on the phone.

"Can you go and check if anything else inside is stolen?" he said. "Then we'll take what we can back with us."

Jimmy disappeared back into the cottage as Sergeant Thornton appeared from the ginnel next to the pub. Natalie was with him and he could hear him explaining what was going on to her.

"Thank you for your help, Sergeant Thornton," he said. "Fortunately, Kemp came quietly. We've arrested him in connection with the burglaries. Various stolen items are in his house. Would you both give Sergeant Chang a hand?"

"Where's Craig now?" asked Natalie.

"He's been taken to York for further questioning about the murder of Kenelm Underhill."

Sergeant Thornton puffed out his cheeks and shook his head sadly. "Well, I can't say I'm surprised. Craig's always been a bit of a troublemaker. Not that I ever thought he'd kill someone. Poor Glenda!"

With that he trotted up the path through the front door, but Natalie hung back. As the sergeant had been speaking, Shadow noticed she had turned the colour of a ripe tomato.

"Is there something you would like to share with me?" he asked when her sergeant was out of earshot.

"Craig couldn't have killed Kenelm Underhill, Chief Inspector. He has an alibi for that night, sir," she replied looking at her feet, then took a deep breath before she continued, "He was with me. All night."

"I see. Are the two of you in a relationship?" asked Shadow.

She looked up and shook her head. "No. God, no." Then she shrugged. "We used to go out when we were kids, back when we were at school. We were both at the pub for the quiz and we'd had a few drinks together and well, I guess it was an old times' sake thing. We left the pub at closing time and went to my place, and he didn't leave until the morning. It was a mistake. I'm sorry, sir, I mean Chief."

"No need for an apology. Your private life is exactly that. I appreciate your honesty, but perhaps it might be better if you weren't involved with removing the stolen items."

The young woman bit her lip but nodded. "I understand. Would it be okay if I nipped inside to let his mum know where he was that night. She'll be ever so worried. He's all she has now."

Shadow nodded and watched her hurry inside. Then he turned towards the Black Bull. He was considering whether he had time for a pint when Trevor Thornton and Reverend Prescott walked out of the door. The two men appeared to be deep in conversation and hadn't noticed him.

"Good afternoon, gentlemen," he said as they got closer. Both men looked up in surprise.

"Good afternoon, Chief Inspector. We were just discussing arrangements for Kenelm's funeral, tomorrow. Trevor is going to be one of the pallbearers as Cedric won't be able to attend," explained the vicar.

"The funeral is tomorrow?" He hadn't realised the body had been released.

"Apparently. Edmund is very keen to lay his brother to rest as soon as possible."

"I see. You must be hoping the funeral doesn't coincide with a visit from the competition judges."

"Indeed, indeed," replied Reverend Prescott and gave a slightly nervous laugh. Beside him Trevor looked decidedly awkward. "Well, we must be going. Lance has been on duty, keeping watch in the churchyard for the last couple of hours. One of us should really relieve him."

Shadow nodded as they moved away. He waited a second before calling after them. "Why didn't either of you tell me you'd been drinking brandy together at Mill House on the night Kenelm was murdered?"

They both froze, then slowly turned around. He would

normally have waited until he had confirmation that the second set of prints belonged to Trevor, but the look on both their faces told him he had been right to confront them.

"What do you mean, Chief Inspector?" asked Reverend Prescott, stuttering slightly, but Trevor laid a hand on his arm.

"We should tell him the truth, Tristram," he said gently, then looked at Shadow. "I'm sorry, Chief Inspector, we should have been straight with you…" he gave a slight smile "…if that's not a contradiction in terms. I came down to the pub on Monday night to see Tristram mainly. We don't get much chance to be together."

"It's not that we are ashamed," added Tristram.

"No," agreed Trevor sounding more definite than he ever had before. "But we knew if Kenelm found out about us, he could make life very difficult. He had very strong views about people like us. I would have lost my job and he'd have made things very difficult for Tristram. Kenelm was church warden and benefice patron. It was really up to him who got to be vicar at St Cuthbert's." He paused. "I know you are probably thinking that gives us a perfect reason to want him dead, but we didn't kill him. When we left the pub, we got fish and chips like I said and ate them on the way to Mill House. We took the path through the church down to the beck then went through the back garden, so the CCTV cameras didn't see us. I could see a lamp on in Kenelm's study so we walked up the path that leads up to the kitchen door."

"Was the study door smashed at that point?" asked Shadow.

Trevor shook his head. "We weren't close enough to see and we didn't hear or see anything that made us think something was wrong, except…" He hesitated and ran his hand over his face.

Tristram patted him on the shoulder as he took up the story. "We went into the kitchen and Trevor poured us both a small glass of brandy. Glenda keeps some in the medicine cupboard. As we sat down, Badger came running through to see us. He was whining and wouldn't settle."

"He must have been trying to tell us something was wrong, but we thought he was just being daft," said Trevor. "I thought his noise might bring Kenelm through, so I sent him out into the corridor and shut the door behind him. If we'd followed him, we might have been able to save Kenelm."

"What time did you arrive in the kitchen?"

"It was a little after midnight. We heard the church clock striking as we walked through the garden. I left after about fifteen minutes and took the fish and chip wrappers with me so Glenda didn't find them. It was when I was putting them in the bin in the churchyard that I noticed the damage around the sundial. You know the rest already. I stayed in the churchyard until the morning and Trevor finished his shift."

Shadow nodded. The two of them sounded convincing but that didn't change the fact that they'd lied to him and had only told the truth when they were challenged.

"You never mentioned that your father had been injured by Kenelm and Lance either, Mr Thornton."

Trevor sighed and shook his head. "That was thirty years ago, Chief Inspector, and it was my grandad not my dad. He's been dead for twenty-five years." When Shadow didn't respond he continued. "He saw them in the car and knew they were off their heads. He went to stop them, to stand in their way, thinking they would break but they hit him."

"Who was driving?"

"They both ran off after the crash, but later Lance admitted it was him. Grandad didn't bear a grudge and always said it was better him, an old man, rather than a child or someone else. For their part, they both apologised and Lance certainly paid for it. He's never had so much as a shandy since and I reckon that's why he's such a fitness freak."

"Which of us wouldn't change something in our past if we could," chimed in Tristram. "We shall forever blame ourselves for not going to Kenelm's study and we didn't have the excuse of youth."

Shadow merely nodded. "I'll need you both to make new statements and would ask that neither of you leave the area without telling us until the investigation is complete." Both men murmured their agreement. They looked so wretched Shadow took pity on them. "Our pathologist tells me that

Kenelm died almost instantly. Even if you had gone through to the study, it is unlikely you could have saved him."

"Thank you," said Trevor quietly as Shadow turned away. He walked across the marketplace to where Jimmy was loading more items from Glenda's house into their car.

"That's the last of them, Chief," he said as he closed the boot. "At least two items from each of the four houses that were burgled. There's no way Craig will be able to explain that."

"Perhaps not, but we aren't going to be able to pin Kenelm's murder on him."

"Yeh, I heard Natalie talking to Glenda. It was a bit awks as Ben and Ollie would say but at least we're making progress. What did Trevor and the rev have to say?"

"When I confronted them, they admitted they had been in the kitchen at Mill House drinking brandy between twelve and quarter past on the night Kenelm was killed. They said Badger seemed distressed, but they ignored him because they didn't want Kenelm to find out about their relationship."

"Did you believe them?"

"I think so. He confirmed it was his grandfather that was run over by Kenelm and Lance too."

"Wouldn't that mean it was Glenda's grandad too and Craig's great-grandad, Chief?"

"Yes, I suppose it would. Shame Craig is out of the picture. Now, let's get up to Mill House and see if we can find this mint tea Glenda threw out."

Jimmy made a face. "That means going through the rubbish bins, right?"

"Hopefully, unless the bin men have beaten us to it."

"What have you done to your hand?" he asked, noticing Jimmy was holding his left wrist at a strange angle as he climbed into the car.

"It's nothing, Chief. I burnt it a bit, that's all. I went to pick up a digital radio from the windowsill and my hand brushed against the kettle that had just boiled. Glenda was really nice though. She put some aloe vera on it."

"Good. We haven't got time to take you to A and E."

A few minutes later, they arrived at Underhill's Mill. The place seemed eerily quiet, then Shadow remembered the workers had been given leave until after the funeral. They knocked on the front door of Mill House but there was no answer.

"Shall we go round the back?" asked Jimmy, but then they heard a voice calling out.

"Hello! Can I help you?" It was Olivia. She came striding towards them from the direction of the stables.

"Good afternoon, Mrs Underhill. Please could you tell us when your rubbish bins were last emptied?" asked Shadow.

Olivia looked surprised. "Last Friday. Why?"

"We understand you asked Glenda to throw away some items from the kitchen. We'd like to take some samples."

"If you mean all those awful concoctions Alice made for him, then Glenda didn't put them in the bin. She threw them on to the compost heap next to the greenhouse in the garden. Kenelm was a keen composter you see, Chief Inspector. Even after he was gone, she would still do what he wanted. Do you mind finding your own way there? I'm in the middle of grooming Ivar, then I want to go for another ride. I won't have chance to tomorrow, with having to go to the funeral."

"I heard your son won't be coming home for his father's funeral," said Shadow as she turned to go. Her pretty face hardened.

"No, he won't, and I don't blame him. I told you before Kenelm had outdated ideas, well I was being polite. If I'd known what a homophobic, misogynistic old racist he was, I would never have married him. His own son crossed an ocean to get away from him."

"Were these homophobic opinions of Kenelm's only in regard to his son or did they stretch to other people in the village?"

Olivia narrowed her eyes a little. "I know first-hand what it's like to have half of Ellerdale gossiping about you. That's another item on a very long list of village activities that I won't join in with. As far as I'm concerned, the private life of anyone who works here has absolutely nothing to do with me. It's a shame Kenelm couldn't see that, instead of thinking as an Underhill, he had the right to be some sort of feudal overlord." Her features softened a little. "Chief Inspector, you may not think our security guard acted very professionally, but I have always found Trevor to be kind, helpful and honest despite how life has treated him. By now, he should have been a captain in the cavalry at the very least, and there's nobody else I would trust to take care of Ivar and Badger when I go away. Now if you will excuse me, Ivar will be getting impatient. He's already got his saddle on."

With that, she headed back to the stables. The two detectives made their way around the side of Mill House and down to the path by the beck then went through the gate into the rear garden. They passed the little rowing boat moored where it had been on the day they first arrived in Ellerdale.

"Let's take the path that leads up to the kitchen," said Shadow remembering what Trevor and Tristram had told him. They set off down the path that ran to the left. Shadow kept glancing up at the house. What Trevor had told him was true. You could see the top row of glass panes in the study door but no more. Jimmy who was leading the way, suddenly stopped next to a pretty wooden arbour.

"Look, Chief. More tab ends."

Shadow knelt down to take a closer look. Beneath the slatted wooden bench inside the arbour were half a dozen cigarette ends. Although most of the printing on the paper had been burnt off, he was fairly certain, from what remained, that they were the same as the ones Ben and Ollie had found up by the memorial.

"Bag them up," he said as he straightened up, feeling a

slight twinge of pain in his back. He wasn't sure whether it was the lack of sleep or this case in general that was making him ache and feel weary. He couldn't remember an investigation when he'd found it so difficult to work out what was important and what wasn't. Even as he watched Jimmy put his hand inside an evidence bag and used it as a glove to scoop up the tab ends, he couldn't be sure they weren't wasting their time. With a sigh, he continued on his way.

The gravel path led them to the far side of the garden, then took them up a fairly steep and twisted incline until they arrived at a small terrace by the rear door that led into the kitchen. There were some wooden planters where someone, Shadow guessed it was Glenda, was growing various herbs and vegetables and in the corner stood a greenhouse. As Olivia had told them, behind the greenhouse was the compost heap enclosed by a stone wall. Shadow and Jimmy peered down on to the rotting heap of grass clippings and vegetable peelings.

"We are never going to find the leaves or whatever they are in this lot," said Jimmy. "Should we get Ben and Ollie to come and take a look? Or maybe we could find an expert herbalist or someone. I could look on the database," he offered as his phone began to bleep.

Shadow shook his head. "Even if someone can identify the pennyroyal, I can't see how they are going to be able to connect it to Alice or anyone else. It looks like we are back to square one as far as the poisoner is concerned," he grumbled as he peered into the greenhouse where Glenda had neatly stacked the labelled wooden boxes that had stored the tea. He noticed she drawn a little picture of each plant too. He was wondering if she had washed them out when Jimmy interrupted his thoughts.

"Actually Chief, we've got another setback. There's a message from the custody sergeant. Craig Kemp has tested positive for alcohol and cannabis. It could be a while before we can interview him."

"Wonderful!" tutted Shadow impatiently. "I should have gone upstairs myself. He was probably getting high in bed while we were waiting to speak to him." He thought for a second. "Right. We might not be able to pin the pennyroyal on Alice but let's see if what she has to say about the plentiful supply of dope in this supposedly perfect village."

However, after they had returned to their car and began the short drive back to the village, Shadow noticed a grey plume of smoke rising into the clear blue sky.

"Looks like someone is having a bonfire," commented Jimmy who must have spotted it too.

Shadow suddenly groaned as he realised which building the smoke was coming from. "Put your foot down. She's getting rid of the evidence. She must have worked out we were on to her."

"Alice? Do you think she had a premonition?"

"I think it's more likely our visit to Craig spooked her. Now get down there."

A few minutes later, they screeched to a halt outside the schoolhouse. They fought their way through the overgrown front garden, but despite hammering on the door for several minutes, there was no answer.

"How do we get into the back garden?" asked Shadow.

"I think we have to go round the school," replied Jimmy, straining his neck to see past the apple trees. They hurried back out on to the pavement and down past the school until they reached the gate that had once led into the schoolyard. It was chained and locked with a padlock and partly obscured by nettles. They managed to avoid getting stung as they climbed over and ran across the potholed yard to the rear of the school. Shadow pointed to a severed electrical cable peeping out of one of the boarded-up windows.

"Evidence for Edmund's exorbitant electric bill," he said.

Jimmy gripped hold of the windowsill, hoisted himself and squinted through a gap in the boards. "Empty inside, Chief." He pulled at the piece of cable as he dropped back down. "This is all that's left. No heaters, lamps and definitely no plants." He dropped the three-inch length of cable into another evidence bag.

Shadow silently kicked himself for not coming here first. At the edge of the schoolyard was an old wooden stile that led into the rear garden of the schoolhouse. Jimmy vaulted over and Shadow clambered after him, his sore back making him even more ungainly than usual.

Standing at the bottom of the garden with her back to

them was Alice. She was wearing dark blue overalls and was poking a long wooden stick into a huge roaring bonfire.

Jimmy exhaled heavily. "She's incinerated the lot."

Shadow nodded in silent agreement. Despite the heady smell coming from the fire, he doubted any plants had survived.

"Is there an extinguisher in the car?"

"Yes, Chief."

"Then go back and get it. That fire needs bringing under control and God knows how many bylaws she's breaking."

Jimmy disappeared back over the hedge and Shadow made his way towards Alice and the fire. As he got closer, he could feel the intense heat and the pungent smell was almost overwhelming. He was only a few feet away when Alice turned around and gave him an innocent smile.

"Hello there, Chief Inspector. What a nice surprise. I'm sorry I can't offer you a cup of tea but I'm a little busy. I don't want this fire getting out of hand." She prodded the flames again with her stick.

"Rather an extreme way of getting rid of evidence," replied Shadow.

"I don't know what you mean, Chief Inspector. I'm simply clearing the garden of a few troublesome weeds that had rather taken hold."

"We have Craig Kemp in custody. He's facing several charges. I understand he's rather a good customer of yours."

In truth, Craig hadn't mentioned Alice, but she didn't

need to know this.

Her face remained impassive. "He must be mistaken. He drinks a lot, you know. Alcohol can do strange things to the mind."

"As can cannabis, Miss Debenham."

"It also has many beneficial qualities. It's terribly good for pain relief, Chief Inspector. You should try it. You seem to be walking a little stiffly."

Her comment only seemed to make the pain in his back worse and it certainly didn't improve his patience.

"That may be true, but it is still an illegal substance. Are you aware that the maximum sentence for supplying or producing an illicit drug is fourteen years? We have found various pieces of evidence that link you not only to the supply of drugs but that the prosecution might find helpful when constructing a case against the killer of Kenelm Underhill."

"I see," she said and was silent for a moment as she poked at the fire again. "I assume Craig, who usually does little more than grunt, suddenly became so talkative in the hope you may look upon his case more kindly. Would I be correct in thinking that if I could also provide you with certain useful information, you may be prepared to forget about my little bonfire?"

"What would this information be?"

"Edmund and Olivia are having an affair. They have been for years."

"Half the village already knows that."

"Trevor and Tristram?" she enquired.

Shadow nodded.

"What if I told you that Lance asked me to lie for him?"

"What about?"

"He didn't arrive back in the village until after midnight on Tuesday night. He should have been back from Durham at least two hours earlier. When I mentioned it, he said if anyone should ask, I should say he was here with me."

Shadow frowned. Why would Lance need to lie about his whereabouts the night after Kenelm was killed? He realised Alice was watching him closely.

She gave an exaggerated shrug of her shoulders. "I don't know why. Perhaps you could ask him."

"Can we agree that this will be your last attempt to cultivate this particular plant?"

"Absolutely, Chief Inspector. I've decided to invest in a greenhouse and grow my own tomatoes and courgettes. I'm going to look into getting a stall on the market."

"That sounds very wholesome if not quite as profitable," he replied, then suddenly remembering what else they had suspected her of, said, "What would you say if I told you that someone had reported seeing you collecting pennyroyal down by the beck?"

Although this wasn't true, he was surprised by her reaction. For the first time since he'd met her, the air of self-confidence had vanished, and she looked genuinely confused.

"I'd say they were either lying or mistaken."

"You do know what it is and agree that it does grow in large quantities by the village beck?"

"Yes…" and her composure returned "…but forgive me, Chief Inspector, the main use of that particular plant was to end unwanted pregnancies, and the days when that subject was of any concern to me are long gone. Perhaps the one and only benefit of the menopause."

The innocent expression was back and now it was Shadow's turn to feel uncomfortable. However, he was saved by Jimmy returning with the fire extinguisher. A few seconds later, the fire was out.

"Thank you, Sergeant Chang," said Alice sweetly. "I would show you gentlemen out, but I feel I should stay and keep watch in case any embers should try to stray."

She turned back to the smouldering pile of vegetation and the two detectives made their way back towards the hedge.

"Aren't we arresting her?" hissed Jimmy.

Shadow shook his head. "No. At least not yet."

After he'd heaved himself back over the stile, he told his sergeant everything Alice had said.

"What did she mean about Lance?" he asked.

"I don't know but I have a feeling it's important."

"But you don't think she's the one who was poisoning Kenelm?"

"No, I don't. When I mentioned the pennyroyal, she

really didn't seem to know what I was talking about."

"Oh well, we now know who was behind the burglaries and who was supplying the dope. We still need to work on who killed Kenelm, who was trying to poison him, if it isn't the same person, and who's been digging up the old churches, but two out of five isn't bad."

Shadow merely grunted in response as he walked back to their car, replaying his conversation with Alice. While he waited for Jimmy to join him and unlock the door, he suddenly had the feeling he was being watched. He raised his hand to shield his eyes from the sun and scanned the buildings surrounding the marketplace. Was that a slight movement in the upper window of Camelot Cottage? He turned to ask Jimmy if he'd seen anything, but his sergeant was crouched down near the schoolyard gate.

"What are you doing?" he asked impatiently.

"Sorry, Chief. I've nettled the hand I burnt earlier. I'm just trying to find some dock leaves."

"Well, hurry up or I'll have to drive us back to York."

He turned back to look at Camelot Cottage but there was nobody there.

CHAPTER NINE

Across 1 (10 letters)
A coin fit for a king

I T WAS EARLY evening when they finally returned to York.
The Brigantes Race had closed the road they usually took
and no amount of chuntering from Shadow about the Lycra-
clad cyclists or the length of the detour got them home any
quicker. Nor was his mood improved when the custody
sergeant informed them that although Craig was now sober
enough to be interviewed, the duty solicitor had been called
away and wouldn't be able to return until the morning and
Craig refused to speak to them without her.

"Then we'll have to interview him first thing," said
Shadow with a sigh. He rubbed a hand over his eyes. "I'm
going to get something to eat, then see if I can catch up on
some sleep."

However, his luck showed no sign of improving when he
arrived at La Scuola Femminile, another of his favourite
Italian restaurants, on Petergate. Francesco greeted him as
warmly as ever but hesitated a little before escorting him to
his usual table.

"I should probably warn you, Chief Inspector, tonight we have two hen parties booked in. Sometimes there is no problem, but sometimes it can get out of hand. They start to sing or try and dance on the tables. Sometimes items of clothing are removed…"

Shadow took in the gaudy foil balloons already decorating two large tables in the restaurant and decided not to risk it. He asked Francesco for a takeaway pizza instead and left just as a large party of twenty-something young women wearing pink cowboy hats arrived. Carrying the insulated bag that held his large pizza, he cut through Shambles and headed to Ouse Bridge then took the steps down to the river. He passed the King's Head where the outside tables were full of people enjoying a pint, now the clocks had gone forward despite the early evening chill.

He walked on by the boats that took tourists on cruises up and down the river. A young man was chalking the times of the evening cruise departures on a blackboard. Shadow stopped.

"Do you hire the rowing boats and kayaks down by Lendal Bridge too?" he asked.

"It's the same company but I think the last time you can hire them is five," replied the young man.

"That's all right," said Shadow, not sure if he should be amused or flattered that the young man thought he'd be capable of navigating the river on either. "I simply wanted to let you know one of your kayaks had come loose and was floating down the river earlier in the week. I tried to catch it, but it was too far out."

The young man nodded. "Yep it happens a lot. Drunks usually untie them for a laugh. I suppose we should be grateful they don't try and get in them. The rowing club returned a stray one yesterday. It had got caught in the weeds. That might be the one you saw. Cheers anyway."

Shadow continued on his way and crossed Skeldergate Bridge to where *Florence* was moored. Feeling ravenous, he flopped down on the sofa and removed the pizza box from its bag. He leant back to enjoy the first slice only to feel something digging in his side. He reached in his pocket and found the busker's CD Jimmy had bought. He flung it on the table and shrugged off his jacket. He demolished the rest of the pizza, only stopping halfway through to pour himself a large glass of wine. When he'd finished both the pizza and the wine, he settled back with his head full of thoughts about the case. He yawned, closed his eyes and the next thing he knew it was morning.

He opened his eyes and groaned. His neck and back were sore from being on the sofa all night, but it was the first time he'd had nearly eight hours' sleep all week. Hoping the jets of warm water would help relieve his aches and pains, he showered and dressed then headed back into the city. Reluctantly, he decided against breakfast at Bettys. Interviewing Craig Kemp had been delayed enough already. As he approached the station, he met Jimmy coming from the other direction.

"Morning, Chief! Guess who I saw at Mum's place last night?" he asked cheerfully.

"I'd really rather you just told me. There's far too much guessing going on as it is."

"Dani Piper. Remember, Tyson Piper's half-sister who works on the currency exchange desk at the bank?"

"Yes, yes, I remember. What about her?"

"Well, she was having dinner with a few friends for her baby shower as it turns out, and she spotted me and came over to say 'hello'."

Shadow popped an indigestion tablet into his mouth and hoped this story would end before the tablet dissolved. Falling asleep immediately after eating a full pizza may not have been the best idea.

"Anyway," continued Jimmy, "Dani said she'd been reading about Kenelm's death online and asked me if I was on the investigating team. I said yes, then she asked was he related to Olivia Underhill. Apparently, she remembered the name. Underhill is a bit unusual, I suppose, but she's also thinking of calling her baby Olivia if it's a girl." Then seeing Shadow's expression, he said, "Anyway, about two weeks ago, Olivia Underhill got two thousand US dollars from her."

"She did say that she and Edmund were planning on going away together." Shadow thought for a second. "It's Kenelm's funeral today. I don't think either of them will try and leave before then. Let's get on and interview Kemp."

However, Tom stopped them at the reception desk. "Morning, Chief. Jimmy. There's a Mr Debenham here to see you. He said it was important."

Lance was waiting for them in one of the interview rooms. He was dressed in a dark suit with a black tie. Shadow assumed he must be planning on heading straight back to Ellerdale for the funeral.

"Good morning, Mr Debenham. I understand you wanted to speak to us," he said as he and Jimmy sat down opposite the schoolteacher.

"Chief Inspector, I apologise for not making an appointment, but I should like to make a confession."

"Go ahead," replied Shadow.

Next to him Jimmy was leaning forward and had his electronic notebook at the ready but something in the way Lance was sitting calmly with his hands clasped in front of him told him that his sergeant was going to be disappointed by his revelation.

Lance cleared his throat. "On Tuesday evening, I trespassed on to the grounds of Whitby Abbey and dug four holes in an area I believed may contain Aldfrith's Hoard. I'm deeply sorry for my behaviour and can only offer my heartfelt apologies and to pay for any damage I may have caused."

It sounded like this speech had been well-rehearsed.

"Why did you do it?" asked Shadow. Jimmy's shoulders had visibly slumped.

"A moment of madness. Perhaps it was the grief of losing my oldest friend. We'd always talked about sharing the treasure if we ever found it. As you know, when I heard someone had dug holes near the sundial at St Cuthbert's, I thought it was Kenelm. However, I believed the map may refer to a larger church. Naturally, I thought of Whitby Abbey and decided to try and find the treasure as a tribute to my old friend and, well, as I said, I made a foolish mistake."

"I see. I take it you didn't find anything."

Lance gave a half-smile and shook his head. "No. To be honest, when I had dug the four holes, I realised how foolish I was being and went home. The next morning, I heard that the treasure had been found at St Cuthbert's after all. Although I can't imagine why Kenelm left it there." He paused for a moment. "I was rather hoping you could see your way to not taking this any further. If I was charged with trespass or criminal damage or whatever, well, I'd lose my job, Chief Inspector."

Shadow knew this was probably true and that according to the strange terms of his father's will, he could possibly lose his house too.

"How did you get home?" he asked.

"By bike. I'd gone up to Durham on the train to retrieve my bike. You recall I told you I left it behind in my panic when Alice called about the break-in."

"You don't drive at all?"

"No. I cycle whenever possible or use public transport. I

have a rover pass here on my phone. I use it to go all over with Northern Trains whenever I am home." He showed the screen of his phone to the detectives. Jimmy nodded but Shadow hadn't finished.

"You live and work in a remote rural location. Wouldn't it make more sense to drive?"

"I believe my choices are better for both my health and the environment, Chief Inspector. However, in my youth, I was involved in an unfortunate incident. An elderly man was injured and afterwards, I promised my father I would never get behind the wheel of a car again."

He had confirmed what Trevor had said. Shadow nodded and moved on.

"We had a report of someone digging in the ruins of St Mary's Abbey in the Museum Garden's here in York on Monday evening. You wouldn't happened to know anything about that?"

"No, Chief Inspector. I was in Durham on Monday as you know. Although I understand Tristram and Kenelm were in York recently. Have you asked Tristram?"

"We'll be continuing with our inquiries. Thank you, Mr Debenham. I don't think we'll be taking this any further."

Lance looked visibly relieved. He shook both Shadow and Jimmy by the hand.

"Thank you. Thank you very much."

"Would you be surprised to know that the map Kenelm

found was a fake?" said Shadow as he stood to hold the door open. For the first time, since meeting him Lance looked confused. It reminded Shadow of the expression Alice had worn when he'd mentioned the pennyroyal. The Debenhams weren't used to being wrong-footed.

"A fake," Lance almost stammered, "I don't understand."

"We asked the experts at York university to examine it and they confirmed that although the parchment is from the Anglo-Saxon era, the map has been drawn with modern ink."

Lance stared at them both blankly for a beat before recovering himself. "For the first time, I'm pleased Kenelm isn't here. The disappointment would have been very difficult for him to bear." He paused. "The treasure that Tristram and Alice found at St Cuthbert's?"

"Oh that's genuine enough. Although we haven't got a precise date for it."

"I don't understand," he almost whispered. Despite himself, Shadow was rather enjoying the look of bewilderment on his face.

"No, Mr Debenham. Neither do we. Thank you for coming. We won't keep you. I believe Mr Underhill's funeral is later today."

"Yes. I must hurry to catch the train." Still looking perplexed, he turned and left.

"You didn't ask him about getting Alice to lie for him," said Jimmy as they listened to his footsteps echo down the corridor.

"No, but I think us visiting her yesterday is what prompted his confession. He didn't trust her not to say anything and he was right. I thought it was more interesting that he didn't ask if it was Craig who had broken into his cottage. He must have heard that we have arrested him."

Then right on cue Jimmy's phone bleeped. "Speak of the devil! His brief's arrived."

"Good. Let's see what he has to say for himself before our twenty-four hours are up."

A night in the cells had done nothing to improve Craig's appearance or attitude. He was even more bleary-eyed, dishevelled and belligerent than when they had arrested him. In contrast, his solicitor looked as eager and alert as a terrier watching out for a rat. Jimmy began to list the items they had removed from the Kemps' house and also produced the joint now in an evidence bag that had been removed from his pocket.

Craig barked out a laugh when he saw it. "Come on! I don't need to weigh that to know it's not enough to charge me with possession."

"Where did you get it from?" asked Shadow wondering if he would name Alice.

"I thought you would have worked that out by now," he countered.

"My client understands the seriousness of the crimes he is under arrest for and is keen to cooperate in any way he can," interjected the solicitor smoothly.

"If that's the case, why didn't you tell us you had an alibi for the time Kenelm Underhill was killed?" asked Shadow.

Craig shrugged. "I wasn't sure if I did. I didn't know if Natalie would back me up."

"She's confirmed that the two of you were together from the time the pub closed until six o'clock the following morning."

"Good of her," grunted Craig in what Shadow thought might be another contender for the understatement of the year. He found it interesting that, so far, he had remained loyal to both Natalie and Alice. His alibi was also clearly news to the solicitor who looked a little put out.

"Is that all you have to say regarding the murder of your employer?"

Another shrug.

"Would you rather return to discussing the spate of burglaries and the amount of stolen property we found at your home address?"

"That is why my client has been arrested," said the solicitor, trying to regain the upper hand.

Craig didn't seem to hear her. Instead, he leant forward. "No. Why don't we discuss the people who live in my village, and you can tell me if what I say might cancel out whatever it is you found. Murder trumps theft right, Chief Inspector?"

"What do you want to tell me?" asked Shadow.

"On Monday night, I was sat outside the pub having a smoke. It was about eight-ish and I saw Olivia and Edmund driving through the village towards the mill. Going like a bat out of hell they were. Ten minutes later, they came tearing back."

Shadow nodded. Olivia and Edmund had told him they'd left the mill in separate cars at between half past six and seven, but the Greek couple at the restaurant also said they had been late for their reservation. However, all he said was: "We'll look into it."

"Wait, there's more. I heard the deadly Debenhams arguing."

"The deadly Debenhams?"

"Alice and Lance. They both give me the creeps, and she's always been a right cow to Mum. Our family have been in the village just as long as they have. Bloody snobs the pair of them."

"When did you hear them arguing?"

"Late Tuesday night. Lance had cycled round to Alice's. I was going there to get, well it doesn't matter why I was there, but I was outside, and I heard them arguing. She said, 'What's it worth?' and he said, 'You already helped yourself to fifty pounds.' She said, 'It'll take more than that to keep me quiet,' then he said, 'Don't threaten me, Alice. If you try and make life difficult for me, I can make it difficult for you; in fact I already have done.'"

"Then what?"

"Nothing. It sounded like he was getting closer to the door so I scarpered."

Shadow glanced over to check Jimmy had noted everything down. He had a feeling they might be finally getting somewhere but all he said was: "Now if we could return to the burglaries."

Craig sighed as he leant back in his chair. "I was only trying to get my mum some nice things. She works like a slave and she's cleverer than the lot of them put together."

"Are you admitting to the offences?"

"May I have a moment with my client?" The solicitor was looking decidedly ruffled that Craig wasn't following the script they had agreed to.

He continued to ignore her. "I didn't hurt anyone and it's a first offence, so if I admit it, I get—what—a year? Serve six months."

"Possibly," replied Jimmy and the solicitor in unison.

Craig kept looking at Shadow. "And you'll tell them I cooperated?"

Shadow nodded.

"All right then, I can handle six months. So can Mum."

Shadow and Jimmy stood up.

"You'll be charged and then released on bail. You'll need to surrender your passport and attend your local police station once a week. I'll send the custody sergeant through with the charge sheet."

He and Jimmy left Craig with his solicitor.

"Do you think he was telling us the truth about Olivia and Edmund and Alice and Lance?" asked Jimmy.

"Yes, I do." He checked his watch. "The funeral will be taking place now. We'll call Edmund when it's over and ask him about returning to the village on Monday night."

"You don't think we should go over there? You know in case they plan to do a runner."

Shadow shook his head. "I don't think he's the doing a runner type."

"What about that argument he heard between Lance and Alice? Was that about him getting her to cover for digging up the abbey?"

"I wish I knew," he murmured. "Are you okay sorting out the paperwork for Mr Kemp? I'm going to get something to eat."

Five minutes later, Shadow was sitting in the Guy Fawkes Inn. He ordered a steak pie for lunch and turned straight to the crossword in the *Yorkshire Post*. He was hoping it might distract him from the investigation and help clear his thoughts at least for a few minutes. However, the first clue he read was: *With extra time this Saxon partly assists at church*. It seemed he couldn't escape the Saxons no matter how hard he tried. As he filled the squares with the word *sexton*, he paused. Glenda's father had been the sexton at St Cuthbert's. Alice had been quite dismissive about it, calling him the gravedigger. Craig had said she'd treated Glenda badly. The more he thought about the group of friends who had grown up in the village together, the more something jarred in his mind. It was the way they behaved and spoke. They were all his age or older yet their behaviour was quite juvenile. Except Kenelm none were married, and Glenda was the only other one to have a child. Both Lance and Kenelm's lives seemed to have been ruled by their fathers. What had the solicitor said? If Lance besmirched the family name, he lost his home. The way the group sometimes expressed themselves was almost childish too. "Edmund was telling Alice off." "Kenelm wouldn't share it." "Glenda's always been a tell-tale." He'd been thinking that ancient history was the motive for killing Kenelm, but could it be more recent history?

After lunch he returned to the incident room. Jimmy was sitting at a computer sipping one of his expensive takeaway coffees.

"Has Kemp been released?"

"No, Chief, we're waiting for Glenda to bring in his passport. We left a message for her, but she will be at the funeral." He paused. "The more I think about what Craig said about seeing Edmund and Olivia, the more I think we should have gone to the village. There's a chance Donaldson could have got the time of death wrong by an hour or so."

"They didn't show up on the CCTV and Trevor didn't mention seeing them."

"I know but still…"

"All right, we'll call him and ask him about it."

But as Jimmy began dialling the number on his mobile, Shadow noticed Ben and Ollie had arrived. Shadow quickly dug his phone out of his pocket. "Hold on. I'll call him on my phone. You can deal with those two."

His sergeant did as he asked, and Shadow held the now ringing phone to his ear while Jimmy crossed the room. The phone went to voice mail. Shadow left a message and asked Edmund to call him as soon as he could. When he looked up, Jimmy and the two scientists were heading over. He sighed. It looked like he couldn't avoid them after all.

"What brings you two here?" he asked.

"Soil samples," replied Ben.

"More particularly, soil samples and their levels of acidity," added Ollie.

Shadow held up his hand. "I've just eaten. If this is going to be a lecture about decomposing bodies, can it wait for another time? The one thing I can safely say about Kenelm Underhill is that he wasn't buried until today."

"No but that Anglo-Saxon treasure was, Chief."

"It's those soil samples we're taking about."

"Whatever it is you're talking about, can I have it in mono not stereo? Ollie, off you go."

"Well, Chief, here in the UK, acid soil is more widespread than alkaline soil. It's found all over from the Cairngorms to Dartmoor and the Yorkshire Dales and the North York Moors including in Ellerdale. Now while we did find traces of acidic soil on the gold items you brought to us, we found more alkaline."

"So they were buried somewhere else in alkaline soil?" asked Jimmy who was looking as confused as Shadow felt.

"We think so."

"So where can we find alkaline soil?" asked Shadow.

"Chalky areas like the South Downs or the Chiltern Hills."

He thought for a moment then turned to Jimmy. "We should check what the area around Lance's school is like." Then as another thought struck him: "What would it be in Ireland? Any idea?"

"Acidic too, I think, Chief," supplied Ben.

"And here in York?" asked Shadow. "Isn't it clay?"

"That's right but still acidic I think."

"And Whitby would be the same?"

"Probably. I mean we can check to be sure."

"Do that. I'm thinking specifically of Museum Gardens and the area around Whitby Abbey. Let me know if either turn out to be alkaline. Is there anything else? Have you found out where that blue piece of thread you found in the monument came from?"

The two scientists hesitated and exchanged an awkward look.

"Actually, we might have messed up there, Chief," began Ollie.

"It probably came from me. It turns out it was Lycra and a match for the cycling shorts I was wearing that day."

"We'd changed our protective suits after being down by the stream and there's a chance the thread came off…"

"Yes, all right. It can't be helped and as I said at the time it might not be important," replied Shadow trying not to think of the time they must have wasted. "Just let me know about the soil. And those cigarette ends."

The two scientists left the incident room looking dejected. Shadow turned his attention back to Jimmy who was tapping away at his computer keyboard.

"The Chiltern Hills cover Buckinghamshire, Hertfordshire, Bedfordshire and Oxfordshire, including the village near the school Lance teaches at." He shook his head. "I don't get it. I thought we were working on the assumption Kenelm had been digging at St Cuthbert's. Do you think Lance could have found that treasure down south and then buried it in his local church? Why? And what about the map?"

"He admitted to digging in Whitby. We've always thought it was the same person who was digging at St Cuthbert's and in Museum Gardens too," said Shadow more to himself than his sergeant.

"But he was in Durham on Monday night. Chief."

Shadow sighed as the thoughts that were trying to form in his head kept swirling around and refused to come together.

"I've been thinking about the case we had at Kirkdale. Do you remember when that horse trainer rode from another moorland village to York and killed that Irish jockey?"

"Yes, what about it?"

"Is there any way Lance could have got back from Durham on Monday night, for example by cycling?"

"No. He left his bike there and he doesn't drive."

"He could have taken the train or the bus."

Jimmy shook his head. "He might have been able to get back to York or Whitby, but I doubt there are any late-night buses to Ellerdale and if he'd been on one someone would have seen him."

"Could he have stolen or rented a bike?"

Jimmy began to smile.

"What?" asked Shadow irritably.

"If I'd come up with this theory, you'd have told me it was far-fetched. In fact, you would probably have said worse. I know you aren't keen on the Debenhams, Chief. But Lance can't have been in two places at once."

Shadow frowned. His sergeant was probably right, but he still kept coming back to the fact that Lance seemed to be the only one as obsessed with the Anglo-Saxon treasure as Kenelm was.

"Contact Durham station and see if you can look at their CCTV footage after about five o'clock on Monday evening. Check the bus station too." Then as an afterthought, "Get Tom to check up on the reports of that motorbike that was heard near Museum Gardens too."

"Tristram?"

"It would be easier for him to have buried those items in his churchyard than anyone else and we know he was up at the Mill House."

Jimmy has looking uncomfortable again. "I know what Ben and Ollie said was interesting and everything but even if we found out who buried the treasure at St Cuthbert's it doesn't mean they murdered Kenelm too. Does it?"

"No," admitted Shadow, "but it feels like it's another loose end we might be able to tie up. If we do, it might take us a step closer to finding our killer." He jumped a little at the unfamiliar sound of his own phone ringing. He squinted at the screen. "Speaking of which. Your number-one suspect is calling me back. I'll take it in my office."

"Hello, Chief Inspector Shadow speaking," he said as he headed out of the noisy incident room and up to the peace and quiet of his office.

"Shadow. Edmund Underhill. You do know it's my brother's funeral today?"

"Yes. I apologise for the intrusion, but I wanted to ask you why you returned to Ellerdale on Monday evening and why you didn't tell us about it."

"I don't know what you are talking about." There was a pause. "Oh hold on! Yes, we did return, but for less than a minute. Olivia had left her passport in the stables of all places. We went back to collect it. I didn't even get out of the car."

"Why did she need her passport so urgently?"

"She needed it to apply for the ESTA Visa Waiver for when we go to the USA. Olivia isn't the most organised of people and had forgotten all about it."

"When were you planning on going to the USA?"

"Actually, we should have been flying out today hence the need to get the visa sorted. Obviously, after what happened we had to postpone. Olivia was upset but Ric told her he could rearrange the party."

"What party would this be?"

"His engagement party. Homer proposed to him on Valentine's Day." Shadow heard him sigh at the end of the line. "Another child saddled with an unfortunate name. Perhaps that's what brought them together."

"So, this trip has been planned for some time?" asked Shadow thinking about the dollars Jimmy had told him about.

"Yes, it was meant to be a double celebration. The engagement and the sale of our shares in the mill. New beginnings all around. Olivia did tell you we planned to go away."

"Is the sale still going through?"

"Oh yes it will be for the entire company now, but there will be a slight delay. Previously, it was only Olivia, Cedric and me selling our shares. Now we can include those owned by Kenelm and Lance."

"Didn't Lance want to sell his before?"

"He did. Very much. It would have meant he could have

given up teaching those brats as he calls them, but his shares are subject to a clause. He can only sell to the chairman of the company and Kenelm wouldn't buy them. I believe our father wanted to ensure the shares couldn't be sold to anyone outside the family. He could be rather controlling as could Lance's father. A different generation and all that."

"Now you are chairman, Lance can sell to you?"

"Absolutely and we'll get a much better price if we can sell the whole company."

"I see. Thank you very much."

Shadow ended the call and began pacing up and down in front of the window. Below him one of the cruisers taking tourists up and down the river chugged by. He thought about what Edmund had told him. Maybe Jimmy was right. If they wanted to find out who killed Kenelm, they should forget all about the Anglo-Saxon treasure he had been so obsessed with. Right on cue there was a knock at the door and Jimmy appeared.

"News from Durham Station, Chief."

"Yes."

"They have footage from Monday evening, but the guy I spoke to actually laughed when I told him we were looking for a middle-aged white man dressing in cycling kit. It turns out at least three cycling groups from the north-east were heading to Yorkshire on the same train to take part in the Brigantes Race."

"So, Lance could have been on the train to York?"

"Yes, but so were at least fifty other middle-aged white men wearing Lycra and cycling helmets. They're sending the footage over. I'll let you know if we see anything."

He disappeared and Shadow began pacing again, deep in thought as an hour ticked by. Suddenly, he stopped in front of his filing cabinet. The calendar on the wall above it was still on the page for the previous month. It had been a gift from Jimmy and had been sold in aid of a local cat-rehoming charity. Shadow had a feeling his sergeant might be the charity's best customer. Rose had a similar calendar hanging in the kitchen and there was another one behind Maggie's counter. He flipped over the next page that showed a collection of ginger and grey kittens playing with a ball of string. They reminded him of the cats at Ellerdale.

Then, with a start he realised he'd missed it. The first of April was Luisa's birthday. They'd always made a joke about it. For the last twenty-five years he'd always dreaded it coming around, but this year he'd forgotten all about it. He stood staring at the small square, then grabbed his old wax jacket and headed out the door.

He crossed St Helen's Square and turned left on to Blake Street, then dodged by the taxis waiting on Duncombe Place before stepping inside St Wilfrid's, the city's largest Catholic church. It was empty, cool and dark. Silently, he lit a candle and stood for a moment, letting the peace and quiet wash over him. Then he whispered "Happy birthday. I didn't forget, I've just had a lot on my mind," before turning and walking back outside. He paused for a moment, blinking in the bright afternoon sun.

"Been confessing your sins?"

He looked round and saw Maggie smiling up at him.

"More like looking for divine intervention," he replied.

"Oh dear, not making much progress?"

Shadow shook his head. "It feels like trying to do a jigsaw with half the pieces missing. We made an arrest for the burglaries, but the culprit has an alibi for the two break-ins at Ellerdale. We know who was supplying Kenelm with cannabis but not who was poisoning him or who killed him. Oh and we know who was digging for Alfred's Hoard in Whitby but not here in York, or at the church in Ellerdale."

"Didn't you say you thought the same person was responsible for all the digging?"

"Yes, but he was about eighty miles away at the time." He sighed. "I thought a walk might help clear my head."

She fell into step beside him as they strolled towards Lendal Bridge.

"Actually, I'm pleased I bumped into you. I've decided to hold a little get-together for Sam and Paloma when they arrive at the weekend. I thought it would be a nice way for her to meet the family."

"All of them?" Maggie had more brothers, sisters, cousins, nieces and nephews than he could count.

"Why not? She's from a big family too. I met all her relatives last time I was out there." She paused. "You can come too if you want. Or will you be too busy?"

The overly casual way she asked and the way she'd already given him an excuse, told him this was important to her. She knew he hated parties and she continued to stare straight ahead as she waited for his reply.

"Of course I'll come. It'll be good to see Sam again and to meet Paloma," he said trying his best to sound genuine. "But don't expect me to make small talk or remember everyone's names."

He was rewarded with a grin as she linked her arm through his.

"I'll get them to wear name badges. Actually, that's not a bad idea, for Paloma's benefit if not yours."

They had drawn level with the little delicatessen in one of the bridge's old toll houses. They sold prepacked picnic hampers for tourists to enjoy in Museum Gardens or to take with them if they were venturing out of the city.

"Why don't we take one of those back to *Florence*?" he suggested.

"My goodness. Social and spontaneous. A case should have you stumped more often."

CHAPTER TEN

Down 8 (4 letters)
Oils in the earth can't be a good thing

THEY CROSSED LENDAL Bridge arm in arm and walked along the river back to *Florence*. Once on board, Shadow opened a bottle of wine while Maggie unpacked the cheeses, French bread and salad from the hamper whilst complaining about the lack of crockery in the galley. As it was still light, they went outside to eat, sitting on the wooden benches at the front of the boat and trying to ignore the geese edging closer and closer along the roof, their sharp eyes fixed on the crusty bread. However, they were saved from an avian ambush by a sharp and sudden downpour. Gathering everything together they hurried inside with what was left of the picnic. Shadow dumped their plates in the sink and refilled their glasses as Maggie finished nibbling the last piece of stilton.

"What's this?" she asked picking up the busker's CD.

Shadow tutted. He had forgotten all about it. "Jimmy bought it. I should have thrown it overboard."

"I didn't have him down as a folk music fan."

"He isn't and he doesn't own a CD player, but he's always wasting his money on something: coffee, trainers. Actually, I think he bought it for me. He probably thought if he got me to listen to it, I'd get used to it and stop complaining when the pirate captain played outside my office. There's more chance of me going deaf."

"Come on, let's have a listen. It can't be that bad. I know 'The Wild Rover' and 'Scarborough Fair'," replied Maggie going over to the CD player. Shadow winced as a few seconds later the sound of the jaunty accordion filled the air. At first Maggie began swaying along in time, but after listening to the first two tracks in silence, even she was wearing a pained expression and Shadow had opened another bottle of wine.

"Okay, I take your point," she admitted, finally pressing stop. "But look, there's a leaflet in the CD cover. It tells you all about the stories behind the songs." She settled next to him on the sofa and began to read. "'Little Musgrave and Lady Barnard'—Musgrave has a secret lovers' tryst with her ladyship, but her husband returns home and kills them both. 'Lord Randall'—tells his mother he has been poisoned by his lover. She made him a meal of eels and he realised she had poisoned him on the way home, when his dogs, who had eaten the scraps dropped dead. Oh dear. It's depressing even without the music." She sighed, placing the CD cover on the table and picking up the photo of Alice and Kenelm's engagement instead.

"Is this the man who was murdered?"

"Yes, it was taken about thirty years ago. He'd just got engaged."

"He looks happy. What a shame she dumped him for the hunky Irishman. Who's the handsome chap with the champagne? He looks fun."

"That's Kenelm's brother."

"And the glum-looking girl?"

"Glenda. Do you think she looks glum?"

Maggie scrutinised the photo a little longer. "No, shocked might be a better description than glum. Who took the photo? One of their parents?"

"I don't know," replied Shadow putting his glass down and taking the photo from her. An idea was starting to come together in his head. "I should probably find out. Do you mind if I make a call?"

"No of course not. Although I've never been sure you knew how to use that mobile of yours. I thought you only carried it so Jimmy could keep tabs on you."

"That's not far from the truth," he admitted. Relieved that the number he needed to call was the last one he'd dialled, he pressed the redial button.

"I'll leave you to it," said Maggie. She stood up and kissed him on the cheek before whispering, "Thanks for supper. Good luck."

She disappeared through the door at the same time Edmund answered abruptly.

"I hope this is a phone call telling me you have arrested Kenelm's killer and that we are free to fly to New York."

"Not quite. I have a question for you regarding a photograph."

"What photograph?"

"The one that was taken on the day Alice and Kenelm got engaged. You are in it, as is Glenda, but who took it? Was it Lance?"

There was a pause at the end of the line. "Do you mean the one taken up at Alfred's Monument? It used to be on Kenelm's desk."

"That's the one. Do you remember who took it?"

"Yes. It was Trevor."

"Trevor not Lance?"

"Correct. Lance had been with us, but he'd gone off in a huff."

"Do you recall why? Didn't he approve of the engagement?"

"I don't think that was the reason. He and Kenelm were arguing a lot at the time. It wasn't long after the magic mushroom incident."

"The what?"

"I'm surprised you haven't heard about it. Kenelm and Lance were both home from university. Alice gave them some hallucinogenic mushrooms to try. Anyway, they got completely off their heads, wrecked half the village and only stopped when Kenelm ran over Trevor and Glenda's grandfather."

"Kenelm was driving?"

"Yes, although Lance took the blame. Kenelm already had a caution for being caught with dope, you see. They both got away with it thanks to Dad pulling a few strings," continued Edmund, "but Lance's father wasn't too understanding. He refused to fund Lance's education anymore and told him he'd have to get a job. I think Lance always felt he was treated unfairly and blamed Kenelm."

"But Lance got his degree," said Shadow, knowing that he wouldn't have been able to teach without one.

"Oh, he'd got his bachelor's but he was aiming for a PhD. He wanted to teach but to him that meant lecturing eager undergraduates on the subtle differences between the Jutes, Angles and Saxons not attempting to get a bunch of spotty kids to memorise the tributaries of the Thames every year. Things weren't great between him and Kenelm for a while, but they eventually got over their differences. Ironically, the situation seemed to improve when Alice buggered off to Ireland."

"If Trevor and Glenda were happy to celebrate Kenelm's engagement, I assume they didn't bear a grudge about what happened to their grandfather."

"Oh, Glenda would forgive Kenelm anything and Trevor was probably only there to keep an eye on her. I think he thought Kenelm, Lance and Alice were a bad influence. Now if that's everything, Chief Inspector. It's been a long and trying day."

"Of course. Thank you for your time," murmured Shadow. The line went dead but his mind was already elsewhere. He stepped outside. The rain had stopped, and he could make out Maggie's departing figure crossing Skeldergate Bridge. Farther in the distance, he could see Ouse Bridge and beyond that the Guildhall that was now the police station. He recalled Dr Shepherd explaining to Jimmy how in Anglo-Saxon times the city would have been built with access to the river in mind and then he thought about what Edmund had told him.

He went back inside and found a tattered, well-thumbed ordnance survey map of the North Yorkshire Moors wedged between the books on his bookcase. He unfolded it and took a few moments to study it. Then he shook his head, perhaps his idea was 'far-fetched' as Jimmy might say. He'd hoped getting away from the office would help him think, but he was worried unhappy memories from his own schooldays were clouding his judgement when it came to Lance, who reminded him of the teachers he had loathed. It didn't help that he was struggling to concentrate because the last song Maggie had insisted on playing was still stuck in his head.

He stretched over to remove the offending disc and replace it with his favourite Frank Sinatra and Count Basie album. As the first strains of 'Pennies from Heaven' began to play, Shadow returned to studying the map and tried to block out the song of a man being poisoned by his lover and another young woman trying to prove her love. At some point, he must have drifted off. As he dozed, he dreamt. Images of Edmund spraying champagne, of cats digging up golden treasure in a pot of pink hydrangeas, then walking by the river where the Lady of Shalott lay submerged as the lost red kayak floated away downstream. He woke up with a start and checked his watch. It was almost five. The memory of what he'd been thinking about the night before slowly came back to him. He picked up his mobile phone and called the station.

"Has Craig Kemp been released?" he asked when he was put through to the custody desk.

"Not yet, Chief. His mother was meant to bring his passport in and collect him. He said she'd be at a funeral so I left her a couple of messages, but she hasn't arrived. He's not kicking up a fuss though. He's still asleep."

"All right let me know if she does," he replied as a feeling of unease crept over him. The next number he dialled was Jimmy's.

"Morning, Chief, where did you disappear to yesterday?" He sounded much brighter than Shadow felt.

"It doesn't matter. We need to get to Ellerdale as quickly as possible."

"Okay, I'll meet you at the station," replied Jimmy without asking for an explanation.

Shadow quickly changed his shirt, brushed his teeth and splashed his face with water, then fifteen minutes later, he was in the station car park. Jimmy arrived a couple of seconds later, still in his running gear.

"Sorry, Chief, I was about go for a jog when you called and didn't have time to change. It sounded urgent."

"I think it might be. I'll explain while you drive."

The city streets were quiet this early in the morning and they were soon on the open road.

"Are we going to arrest Edmund?" asked Jimmy as they sped along.

"No. Glenda. That's hoping she's still alive," replied Shadow. Jimmy gave him a startled looked and slammed his foot down on the accelerator. It was a little after six when they arrived outside Glenda's cottage. The village was quiet. The only sign of life was a tractor trundling through the marketplace. Shadow dashed to the front door and knocked loudly but there was no reply.

"We'll have to go round the back," he said and the two of them hurried down the path by the pub and to the gate that took them to Glenda's immaculate garden. Jimmy was the first to reach the cottage. He looked through the kitchen window and turned to Shadow who was just behind him.

"It doesn't look good, Chief."

Shadow reached the window and saw Glenda slumped at the kitchen table, while Jimmy tried the door. It was unlocked. The two of them hurried inside.

"Call an ambulance," ordered Shadow as he went to help her. Miraculously, she was still breathing. He gently eased her head up from the table, so she was sitting upright in the chair. She was still dressed in black from the funeral and on the table in front of her was a green plant in a plastic pot.

"Glenda! Glenda! Can you hear me?" he asked urgently. She opened her eyes. They were red and swollen. He couldn't be sure if it was from crying or from whatever she'd taken. There also appeared to be a rash around her lips and she was struggling to speak.

"Do we know what she's taken? Is it pennyroyal?" asked Jimmy who was providing the call handler with information.

"It looks like hemlock," said Shadow carefully picking up the plant and putting it on the draining board. "Ask them if there's anything we can give her." He quickly filled a glass of water and took it back to Glenda who was clutching at her throat.

"There's no antidote. It's deadly, Chief," hissed Jimmy. Shadow felt his heart sink. He should have realised this could happen and got here sooner. Glenda gave a strange strangled noise and doubled over in pain.

"Here, have a sip of water," he said gently as he brought the glass to her lips. She manage to straighten up and take a drink.

"I shouldn't be here," she croaked.

"Don't worry. An ambulance is on its way," he tried to reassure her.

"I ate ten leaves. I shouldn't be here. I should be dead. My mouth and throat feel like they're on fire." She reached for the glass, and he held it steady as she gulped down more water.

"There must be something we can do, Chief. Isn't there anything we can give her to make her throw up?" asked Jimmy as he urgently began opening and closing the kitchen cupboards. "Sophie would know what to do. I'll ring her or maybe Ben and Ollie."

"Don't distress yourself, Sergeant," said a calm voice from the doorway. Shadow and Jimmy both turned to see Alice standing there.

"Miss Debenham, will you please wait outside," said Shadow. Her advice was the last thing he needed.

"An ambulance is on its way," said Jimmy as he politely tried to usher her out of the door.

"Oh, there's no need for an ambulance," insisted Alice who was smiling calmly. "That isn't hemlock she's taken. It's fool's parsley. I switched the pots." Both the detectives were staring at her and even Glenda had stopped gasping and groaning. "It's poisonous but not as poisonous as its relative. I expect you are experiencing some burning in the mouth and gullet aren't you, Glenda dear?"

Glenda blinked several times, her hand still clutching her throat. "You switched the pots?" she stammered incredulously.

"Yes. I noticed a pot of hemlock in your greenhouse when I dropped by to see Craig one day." She had the grace to look away when Shadow raised an eyebrow. "I didn't think much about it until I heard about the pennyroyal, then

I realised you might do something silly, especially as it would have been Kenelm's birthday today. I guessed you wouldn't notice. You're not quite the expert your granny was, Glenda."

"I still think she should go to hospital, Chief," said Jimmy who had been busy looking up fool's parsley on his phone.

Shadow nodded. "Go and open the front door for the paramedics and take Miss Debenham with you and get a statement," he replied.

"It's a lot of fuss about nothing," insisted Alice as Jimmy escorted her out of the kitchen. Shadow refilled the glass of water and handed it to Glenda. Her breathing had steadied but she looked confused as she slowly shook her head.

"How did Alice know about the pennyroyal?" she said almost to herself.

"She didn't until I asked her about it," replied Shadow. "We thought, at first, she was trying to poison Kenelm by putting it in the mint tea she made for him. But it wasn't Alice; it was you. Why did you do it? To try and frame Alice? To get rid of her?"

"I kept hoping. I've always loved him. I only got involved with Craig's father because I thought I'd lost him to Alice, then when I came back here, she'd gone, and he'd married Olivia instead. When it was clear things weren't right between him and Olivia, I thought he might turn to me. Then Alice came back." She had a faraway look in her eyes as if she was still talking to herself.

"And you realised he still loved her?" he pressed, and she switched her focus to him.

"She didn't love him though," she insisted, her voice suddenly stronger. "She only used him, but he could never see it. He would believe the world was flat if she told him so."

"Is that why you want to kill him?"

She stared at him, horrified. "I didn't want to kill him, Chief Inspector. You must believe that. I just wanted to look after him. I thought if he became ill. Perhaps needed to take to his bed for a while, then I could take care of him. Nurse him back to health. Alice would stay away. She's never been any good with sickness. She didn't even come home to nurse her own father when he was ill. I thought if he was—what's the word? Incapacitated! That's it. Then Edmund would take over everything. If he was in charge, he wouldn't let Alice stay at the cottage rent-free. She'd have to find somewhere else to live, maybe even go back to Ireland. Edmund and Olivia could be together, and I'd be left in peace to take care of Kenelm."

There was a small eager smile on her face as she explained on this to him, as if it was the simplest thing in the world.

"The doctor who examined Kenelm said the pennyroyal could eventually lead to multiple organ failure."

"Oh, I would never have given him that much. That

morning when I first saw him on the floor, for one horrible moment I thought he'd gone into the kitchen and made himself some tea." She shook her head. "It would have been so out of character. I don't think he even knew how to boil a kettle, bless him. He didn't realise it, but he relied on me completely and I would have done anything for him."

"Like faking that map and hiding it somewhere you knew Kenelm would find it."

"You should have seen his face when he did, Chief Inspector. He looked so happy. He really thought he was about to discover Aldfrith's Hoard at long last."

"Had he lived longer, he might have done. It was you who buried the items near the sundial in the churchyard for him to find. You waited until you saw Tristram leave."

"I knew Kenelm was convinced that's where the hoard was buried and that he wouldn't be able to wait for permission. If he discovered the treasure, it wouldn't matter what the lady at the university said about the map; he'd think he'd made a genuine find."

"Like he believed he'd found all those other items that you buried in his garden and anywhere else you knew he was going to use his metal detector and thanks to your grandfather who took them from the church when he was the sexton you had plenty to keep burying, not to mention the parchment you used to forge the map."

"Grandad didn't steal them, Chief Inspector. You must believe that. He only removed them from the church for safekeeping. He found them in the crypt under the church one day. Old Reverend Debenham—that's Alice and Lance's grandfather—had started helping himself to some of the church's treasures and selling them on. Grandad always said you could never trust a Debenham. He removed the items he found and hid them in our attic for safekeeping. The plan was always to return them, but then I had the idea of letting Kenelm find them instead. It made him happy and avoided having to explain about Grandad keeping his find a secret. The items I buried near the sundial were all that was left."

"But they weren't always in the attic. At some point, you buried them in the pots where you grow your hydrangeas," he said thinking about the large pink plants in the pots at the front of the house.

"That was only recently. I knew the alkaline soil wouldn't damage them too much. I was a bit worried about Craig finding them in the attic, you see. I knew if he did, he would tell me to sell them. That would have spoilt every-thing."

From outside came the sound of the approaching ambu-lance's siren. A few moments later, the paramedics arrived. After explaining what had happened, Shadow left them to do their work and stepped out through the front door.

The arrival of the ambulance had caused quite a stir in the village. The landlord still in his dressing gown was standing in the doorway of the Black Bull. Alice had disap-peared, but Jimmy was now chatting to Natalie, who judging by the way she was dressed was out for a morning run too. Edmund drove by in his sports car. He slowed down but didn't stop. Across the marketplace, he could see Lance cycling towards them. Tristram and Trevor were standing by the church gate. Trevor had Badger on a lead. The poor dog was still looking sorry for himself and had an old leather slipper in his mouth.

Shadow beckoned Natalie over and whispered something in her ear, then said loudly enough for anyone listening to hear, "Sergeant Chang, why don't you accompany PCSO Sharp and help her collect the evidence."

Looking puzzled Jimmy did as he was asked and the two of them jogged away.

"What's going on, Chief Inspector?" asked Lance as his bike came to a halt in front of him.

"There's been an incident involving Mrs Kemp," he explained.

"And you and Sergeant Chang just happened to be here?"

"Actually, we were here to make an arrest. We believe Mrs Kemp may have been trying to poison Kenelm Underhill."

"Good Lord! What with?"

"I have sent Natalie and my sergeant to locate the pennyroyal we think she was using."

Lance tutted. "When will she and Alice stop dabbling with nature's remedies as they insist on calling them? I've always said it would end in tears. It might have been all right in Glenda's granny's day, but the world has moved on since then."

"Quite, Mr Debenham. I also thought it would be kinder if Natalie wasn't here when Mrs Kemp is brought out. I think she will find this difficult enough without being shamed in front of someone she has known since she was a child."

"Point taken," agreed Lance tapping the side of his nose. "I shall also make myself scarce." He cycled back towards his cottage, but Shadow had a feeling he would be following proceedings from there.

There was a noise behind him, and Shadow watched as the paramedics carefully carried Glenda to the ambulance, then sped away with their lights flashing.

Trevor hurried over with Badger. "What's happened to Glenda?" he asked.

"She's ingested a sizeable amount of fool's parsley. The paramedics think it's unlikely there will be any lasting damage but she's been taken to the hospital in Whitby so they can carry out further checks."

Trevor shook his head incredulously. "Poor Glenda! I knew she was upset about Kenelm and about Craig getting arrested, but I didn't think she'd do anything like this. I walked her home after the funeral. I'd never have left her if I'd known. Sometimes I think she should never have come back to this village."

"I should also warn you that when she is released from hospital, we will be arresting her on suspicion of causing grievous bodily harm."

"GBH? Glenda?"

"She was poisoning Kenelm before he died."

Trevor turned pale and shook his head. "Oh dear, oh dear. I'd better get Badger back to the mill then go to the hospital."

Shadow watched him hurry away with Badger, pausing only briefly to speak to an anxious-looking Tristram. Then he headed across the marketplace himself to where, as he'd predicted, Lance was hovering near his cottage gate.

"Poor Badger is still missing his master, I see," he commented. "That's Kenelm's old slipper in his mouth. He was carrying it around with him at the funeral yesterday. Glenda burst into tears as soon as she saw him. It's so very sad. I feel quite sorry for her."

"Even though she had been holding on to the treasure you had been so desperate for all these years?" replied Shadow.

"What?" Lance looked at him in amazement.

"All the Saxon treasure you and Kenelm found over the years and the pieces buried near the sundial. They were all from Glenda. Her grandfather had found Alfred's Hoard years ago in the crypt under the church."

"He didn't tell my grandfather what he'd found?"

"No. It seems he didn't trust your grandfather. Instead,

they were hidden in Glenda's attic until quite recently. You see you didn't need to go skulking around in the middle of the night digging holes at Whitby Abbey and in York's Museum Garden's."

Lance narrowed his eyes. "I confessed to what I did at Whitby Abbey in good faith, Chief Inspector, but I haven't been anywhere near the Museum Gardens."

"Yes, you have. Almost immediately after you checked into your accommodation in Durham, you took the train to York. A train I believe you knew would be packed with cyclists dressed similarly to yourself. You went to Museum Gardens, remained out of sight until it closed, then dug in the location you believed the map Kenelm had briefly shown you gave as the location of Alfred's Hoard. You didn't realise that Glenda with her knowledge of historical architecture had drawn the map on parchment her grandfather had also taken from the church. Then when the warden arrived, you left the gardens by taking one of the kayaks that are left tied up beneath Lendal Bridge. You navigated your way up the river until you reached the beck that runs through the village. That would have taken an experience canoeist like yourself about two hours. By this time, it was around ten thirty.

"You arrived at the jetty outside Mill House, let the kayak float away. You went up to the Mill House and argued with Kenelm. You didn't believe him when he told you he no longer had the map even when you strangled him, then you killed him as you had always planned. You made it look like the place had been broken into. Of course, you couldn't find the map as it was in York, but you took his notebook. Then you hurried to your own house where you also faked a break-in. The noise of people leaving the pub covered the sound of breaking glass. You changed into fresh clothes, dumped some of the items you had removed from the house in the beck and hid out at the monument waiting for the call you knew Alice would make. Then you called the owner of your accommodation in Durham pretending you were still there. You took the boat from the Mill House downstream to Whitby, tied it up near the harbour, then went to the station where you pretended you had arrived by train and took a taxi back to the village."

As Shadow had been speaking, Lance had watching him calmly with his arms folded, his expression growing more and more sceptical. Now he had finished, he began to clap slowly and smiled. "Very good, Chief Inspector. As a piece of creative writing, I would award that an A minus; however, if it was meant to be an essay of historical fact, it would only warrant a D. As an idea it's very interesting but where are the sources to support your theory? I'm sorry, you don't say sources, you say evidence, don't you. Either way it's lacking."

"You told us the last time you saw Kenelm was on Friday morning, but then you mentioned Badger's gate. Trevor installed that gate while you were meant to be away."

"Someone must have mentioned it to me, and it was obvious Badger hadn't been able to protect him, otherwise Kenelm wouldn't be dead," he countered smoothly. "Oh and you haven't explained how I returned the boat to the Mill House. Perhaps it found its own way. Could it have a homing device?"

"You rowed it back from Whitby on Tuesday afternoon, after going there on Alice's bike, which very conveniently folded up. It was a risk as by then we were investigating Kenelm's murder but then using the river at all had been a mistake. I believe you had been planning to kill your old friend for a while, since hearing about the rival company offering to buy the business, in fact. The original plan had you cycling back cross-country from Durham. Timing it to coincide with the Brigantes Race. You would still fake the break-ins and make the calls, but you got greedy when you heard about the map. You wanted to be the one to find the treasure too. You wanted to be famous and regarded highly by scholars to make up for the academic career you had been made to abandon when you and Kenelm were arrested after he persuaded you to take magic mushrooms and the blame for driving that night. You got it into your head that you needed to look in Museum Gardens, but the cycle would hamper you, so you came up with the idea to use the river instead. If only after all your years of studying the Saxons, you and Kenelm had realised the map was a fake."

Lance flinched very slightly. "Again, very interesting but no substance, at least that's what I would say if I were writing your end-of-term report."

"A piece of blue Lycra thread was found at the monument, and we could trace your location using your mobile phone," continued Shadow. He knew he was starting to flounder and by the look on Lance's face so did he.

"I've never liked the idea of signing up for a long contract with a phone company. I prefer the pay-as-you-go option. The boys tease me about it. They call it a burner phone." He was almost laughing at him. Then to his left, but hidden from Lance's view, Shadow saw Natalie and Jimmy appear from their run in the woods. His sergeant gave him a silent thumbs up and Shadow breathed a sigh of relief before turning his attention back to Lance.

"And how can you explain that you were captured walking through the top of the woods on the night Kenelm was killed?"

"Captured how?" asked Lance, his tone no longer so relaxed.

"By the cameras in the badger hide that Sergeant Chang and Natalie have just checked. You must have triggered them as you were going up to Alfred's monument. It was certainly an eventful night."

Lance's face hardened. "We were meant to be friends. I agreed to take the blame for the accident all those years ago, and he promised he would help me while I got my PhD, but then he proposed to Alice and said he couldn't spare any money. She probably put him up to it. He got his doctorate though, didn't he." He gave a sharp laugh. "Even after all these years, he wouldn't help me pursue my dream and buy my shares. The map was the final straw. If he'd shared it with me, if we could have found the treasure together, things might have been different."

His eyes had a faraway look that Shadow found quite unsettling. Then Jimmy arrived at the same time as Sergeant Thornton pulled up in a marked car.

"I phoned him as soon as I saw the recording, Chief," explained a slightly out of breath Jimmy.

"Good. I'll let you do the honours," replied Shadow stepping back as Jimmy took a pair of handcuffs from Sergeant Thornton and began reading Lance his rights.

However, as Jimmy was about to cuff him, Lance's calm façade evaporated and he suddenly yelled, "I am a true Englishman. I will never submit to a foreigner."

He lifted his bike above his head and with impressive agility and balance leapt over the low garden hedge and began pedalling away with Natalie and Jimmy in hot and Sergeant Thornton in lukewarm pursuit. Shadow was about to yell at one of them to take the car, when Lance tried to turn a corner and Merlin the cat suddenly appeared. Lance swerved but crashed into a lamppost and landed in a heap in the ground. Natalie scooped up the yowling cat while Jimmy finally slapped the handcuffs on him.

"Come along now, Lance. Don't make a show of yourself," Shadow heard Sergeant Thornton say as he helped

Jimmy wrestle Lance into the waiting police car.

"How embarrassing! Poor Lance," tutted a voice to his right. He didn't need to turn round to know who it was.

"When did you realise your brother killed Kenelm?" he asked.

"When I went to Mill House on the morning his body was found. The little boat was missing from the jetty, which seemed odd as only Lance and Kenelm ever took it out. Then later when I was leaving it was there tied up with a reef knot. Only Lance used that type of knot. A hangover from his scouting days. That's when I knew he'd been up to something. He's a Scorpio like you, Chief Inspector. I never really trust Scorpios. Now if you will excuse me, we've had word the competition judges are on their way. I've promised to help Tristram show them around and convince them that Ellerdale is the perfect English village."

"Good luck with that," muttered Shadow.

"Oh, now don't sound so cynical, Chief Inspector," she chided. "As far as I'm concerned it is perfect. Especially now. After Lance's transgression, I shall soon be the owner of Camelot Cottage, and all the artefacts dear Kenelm left me will fetch a tidy sum. My future's looking rather rosy."

"You're going to sell his entire collection?"

She gave a catlike smile. "Don't look so shocked. I've always thought being sentimental is overrated." She strolled off humming to herself as the car carrying her brother pulled away.

Jimmy jogged over to where Shadow was standing.

"They're going to take him to York, Chief. I said we'd follow in our car."

Shadow nodded. "First, I want to go back to Glenda's. We need to secure the place and see if we can find Craig's passport so we can release him."

"How did Alice take the news her brother was under arrest for killing his best friend?" asked Jimmy as they crossed the marketplace.

"She knew already. She worked out he had used the rowing boat to get from the village to Whitby before getting a taxi to meet us on Tuesday."

"You're telling me he rowed back all the way from Durham. Is that even possible?"

"No. He took the train to York, which reminds me, we'll need to get some experts to look at the footage from Durham station until they find him and find out what CCTV there is in Whitby harbour. After digging in the ruins in Museum Gardens, he stole a canoe and paddled up here. I spent most of last night checking how the waterways link up and how long it would take him."

Jimmy shook his head. "When you started going on about him cycling back, I thought you were losing the plot."

"Not yet, Sergeant. Actually, I think when Lance planned the murder, he intended to cycle back from Durham, but then the map turned up and he got greedy."

"If it had been left to me, we'd have arrested Edmund."

Jimmy sighed.

"Don't be too hard on yourself. It was your comment about wondering if Alice could have faked the break-in at Camelot Cottage that started me thinking about the burglaries being a red herring. That and the damp laundry and missing boat. But until you found footage of him in the woods, all I had was conjecture."

"Hold on, if Alice knew it was him why didn't she tell us? It can't be because of loyalty. She couldn't wait to tell us he'd asked her to lie."

"I think she was blackmailing him, knowing that she could well be kicked out of her cottage by Edmund and that Lance was going to come into some money when he sold his shares. That was part of the conversation Craig overheard. I think both the Debenhams are scheming, deceitful and as I said greedy. Maybe it's a family trait they inherited from their grandfather. Lance was so penny pinching he only broke or removed items from his cottage that were of low value—and remember the fifty pounds Craig heard him refer to? I think Alice helped herself from the petty cash tin. Lance seemed confused when we mentioned it was missing that first morning."

"Do you think Lance was threatening her when Craig heard him say he would make her life difficult?"

"I think that was to do with the cigarette butts he'd taken from Kenelm's study and left up at the monument. If Ben and Ollie ever get round to analysing them, I'm sure we'll find that Alice had been smoking the ones with traces of lip balm on them. Lance was trying to frame her by linking her to the buried notebook."

"What a family! But even more reason for Alice to come to us. If he got away with murder once, he might try again. And if he could kill his best friend, he could kill his sister too. Especially if she knew he was a murderer."

"I imagine she had some sort of contingency plan in place. Perhaps she was planning on coming to us when she'd wrung him dry. That way she would get his cash and thanks to her father's will, Camelot Cottage too." He gave a wry smile. "She's rather like her description of fool's parsley— poisonous but not as poisonous as its relative."

When they arrived back at Glenda's cottage, Shadow made sure the back door was locked and Jimmy soon located Craig's passport in a small bureau in the sitting room. He pointed to the answer machine with its flashing red light on the desk.

"It looks like she didn't even get the message about coming to the station," he said. "You've got to feel a bit sorry for Craig."

"Oh, I wouldn't give him too much sympathy," replied Shadow as he locked the front door behind them. "All of this may work in his favour. Having a dependent mother, who has recently tried to take her own life could lead to a more lenient sentence."

"That's a bit cynical, Chief."

"I'm only saying what any decent defence barrister with come up with," he said as they climbed into their car. Outside the church they spotted, Tristram and Alice chatting to a group of people holding clipboards.

"It seems the judges have finally arrived," commented Jimmy. "Let's hope for Reverend Prescott's sake they make their decision before news of Lance's arrest hits the papers."

"Alice has probably already taken care of that," murmured Shadow as they set off back to York. "What time is Sophie due back?"

"Actually, I said I'd go up there and collect her. We'd talked about spending the weekend on the Holy Island. I've been reading about it in one of those books Lance gave me, and it means she'll be nearby for a couple more days if her mum and dad need her, but we can do it another time."

"No, it sounds like a good idea. You get off as soon as you drop me off at York."

"Are you sure, Chief?"

"Absolutely, I can sort all the paperwork out and the sooner Sophie is back with us the better."

"There'll be loads to do. It will really muck up your weekend."

"It's fine. I don't have any plans." He paused. "Except for going to a small get-together to celebrate Sam coming home."

"You're going to a party! You hate parties!"

"It's not a party. Just a family gathering."

"If it's Maggie's family, it will definitely be a party."

The Morgan sports car zoomed past them beeping its horn. The back seat was piled high with luggage and Olivia was in the seat next to Edmund, smiling and waving.

"Looks like they're more than happy to leave the village behind, no matter how perfect it is," said Jimmy.

Shadow returned Olivia's wave. "I think it's the past they're leaving behind and I for one don't blame them. It's time for everyone to move on."

The End

AUTHOR'S NOTE

A Saxon Shadow is a work of fiction, but it does include some real places that I used for inspiration. Not far from where I live are St Hilda's at Ellerburn and St Gregory's at Kirkdale, two beautiful Saxon churches that were the inspiration for St Cuthbert's in Ellerdale. Whitby Abbey now lies in ruins but was once one of the largest and most important religious sites in the Anglo-Saxon Kingdom of Northumbria. Today you can still visit the abbey. If, unlike Shadow, you climb up the one hundred and ninety-nine steps, you are rewarded with a wonderful view of the town and harbour. The ruins of St Mary's Abbey in Museum Gardens, York, are also worth a visit. While there, you can also drop into the Yorkshire Museum where you can see the Gilling sword I refer to. The sword was discovered in 1976 by nine-year-old Garry Fridd in Gilling West, North Yorkshire.

The legend of Alfred's or Aldfrith's Hoard is also made up for the purpose of this story but was inspired by King Alfred's Cave, in Ebberston. In 705AD, a great battle took place in the fields between the villages of Allerston and Ebberston. The defeated King Alfred of Northumbria was taken to a hill above the battle, where he later died. In 1790, a monument known as Alfred's Cave was built in his memory. Although the king and battle are long forgotten the monument remains and even today the field where the battle took place and the beck that runs through it are known as the 'Bloody Field' and the 'Bloody Beck'.

Acknowledgements

Thanks so much to everyone at the incredible Tule Publishing:

Jane Porter, Meghan Farrell, Cyndi Parent, Mia Gleason, Kelly Hunter and Julie Sturgeon.

I am very lucky to work with an amazing team of editors who offer endless advice and encouragement.

Huge thanks to Sinclair Sawhney, Helena Newton and Marlene Roberts, who manage to bring some sense and order to all my ramblings.

Many thanks also to Lee Hyat and Patrick Knowles for coordinating and designing such a perfect cover.

A Saxon Shadow Crossword

1.								2.		//// ////	//// ////
//// //// //// ////	//// //// //// ////	//// //// //// 3.	//// //// ////	//// ////	//// ////	//// ////	//// ////		//// //// ////	//// //// //// ////	//// //// //// ////
4.						//// ////	//// ////		//// ////	//// ////	//// ////
//// ////	//// ////	//// ////		//// ////	//// ////	//// ////	//// ////		//// ////	//// ////	5.
//// ////	//// ////	6.				//// ////	//// ////		//// ////	//// ////	
//// ////	//// ////	//// ////		//// ////	//// ////	////	7.			//// ////	
//// ////	8.	//// ////		//// ////	//// ////	//// ////	//// ////		//// ////	//// ////	
//// ////		//// ////		//// ////	//// ////	//// ////	//// ////		//// ////	//// ////	
9.				//// ////	//// ////	//// ////			//// ////	//// ////	
//// ////		//// ////	//// ////	//// ////	//// ////	//// ////	//// ////	//// ////	//// ////	//// ////	
//// ////	//// ////	//// ///	///	10.							

Across

1. A coin fit for a king (10 letters)
4. Canute and Hilda double up with Unwin and Ric in this place of worship (6 letters)
6. Care who wins in this competition of speed (4 letters)
7. Reverse Pam to help you find your way (3 letters)
9. Did Ralph rive this waterway? (5 letters)
10. Lance brings the reed and ivy to me (8 letters)

Down

2. Germanic settlers were lax when they sang at noon (10 letters)
3. Initially, Alfred is sure the rat is valuable (8 letters)
5. Lug Barry along to break-in and take something that isn't his (8 letters)
8. Oils in the earth can't be a good thing (4 letters)

A SAXON SHADOW CROSSWORD SOLUTION

1. P	E	N	N	Y	R	O	Y	2. A	L	////	////	////
////	////	////	////	////	////	////	////	N	////	////	////	////
////	////	////	3. T	////	////	////	////	G	////	////	////	////
4. C	H	U	R	C	H	////	////	L	////	////	////	////
////	////	////	E	////	////	////	////	O	////	////	////	5. B
////	////	6. R	A	C	E	////	////	S	////	////	////	U
////	////	////	S	////	////	////	7. M	A	P	////	////	R
////	8. S	////	U	////	////	////	////	X	////	////	////	G
////	O	////	R	////	////	////	////	O	////	////	////	L
9. R	I	V	E	R	////	////	////	N	////	////	////	A
////	L	////	////	////	////	////	////	////	////	////	////	R
////	////	////	////	////	10. D	E	L	I	V	E	R	Y

If you enjoyed *A Saxon Shadow,*
you'll love the next book in….

THE CHIEF INSPECTOR SHADOW SERIES

Book 1: *A Long Shadow*

Book 2: *A Viking's Shadow*

Book 3: *A Ghostly Shadow*

Book 4: *A Roman Shadow*

Book 5: *A Forgotten Shadow*

Book 6: *A Christmas Shadow*

Book 7: *A Stolen Shadow*

Book 8: *A Saxon Shadow*

Available now at your favorite online retailer!

More books by H L Marsay

The Lady in Blue Mysteries series

Book 1: *The Body in Seven Dials*

Book 2: *A Death in Chelsea*

Book 3: *The Mystery of the Missing Frenchman*

The Secrets of Hartwell series

Book 1: *Four Hidden Treasures*

Book 2: *Four Secrets Kept*

Book 3: *Four Silences Broken*

Available now at your favorite online retailer!

About the Author

H L Marsay grew up binge-reading detective stories and promised herself that some day, she would write one too. A Long Shadow was the first book in her Chief Inspector Shadow series set in York. Luckily, living in a city so full of history, dark corners and hidden snickelways, she is never short of inspiration. She has also written The Secrets of Hartwell Trilogy and The Lady in Blue Mysteries. The Chief Inspector Shadow Mysteries have recently been optioned for television.

When she isn't coming up with new ways to bump people off, she enjoys drinking red wine, eating dark chocolate and reading Agatha Christie – preferably at the same time!

Thank you for reading

A Saxon Shadow

If you enjoyed this book, you can find more from all our great authors at TulePublishing.com, or from your favorite online retailer.

TULE

Printed in Great Britain
by Amazon